HUNTER DALTON

When Dalton killed a man, the corrupt lawman Deputy Vaughn pursued him relentlessly, but in Wilmington Point Dalton enjoyed a welcome slice of luck. He came across Dutch Kincaid's Wanted poster and found that the notorious outlaw had been wrongly blamed for Dalton's crime.

So when Dalton was tasked with infiltrating Dutch's gang of bank raiders, Dalton readily accepted the duty. He figured that if he could kill Dutch, he could claim the bounty on Dutch's head, and his own crime would be officially attributed to a dead man.

But Dalton's dangerous task became even harder when he was partnered with a man who had good reason to kill him and even worse, he still had to face a final showdown with his nemesis Deputy Vaughn.

HUNTER DALTON

ED LAW

 CULBIN PRESS

Copyright © 2015, 2017 by Ed Law
ISBN: 9798595745093

Published by Culbin Press.

ONE

"What's your business in Wilmington Point?" the rider asked.

Dalton was still a few miles away from the town so he leaned forward in the saddle and rubbed his jaw while he thought about what answer he should give. He couldn't be honest, as the truth would be sure to lead to trouble.

Some time ago in the town of Harmony he had killed an evil man to save innocent people. As the dead man had been the lawman Walker Dodge, he had been fleeing for his life ever since.

Deputy Vaughn, a man as corrupt as the man Dalton had killed, had taken it upon himself to pursue him. Vaughn had been relentless so Dalton had become tired of being hunted and he had resolved to end his problems by killing the deputy.

He had soon found that hunting the deputy was as demanding a task as evading him, so he had decided to hole up somewhere and wait for Vaughn to find him. Wilmington Point was his chosen place, as the last piece of information he'd gathered was that Vaughn was in the area.

"I'm looking for work," Dalton said with a conversational tone as he drew his horse to a halt.

The rider identified himself as Finnegan O'Doyle and then eyed Dalton with a surly gleam in his eye, but if Finnegan had been intent on causing mischief, Dalton doubted he'd find him of interest. Aside from his horse and the clothes he was wearing, he had only a few dollars.

"What kind of work?" Finnegan asked. "And who are you?"

"I can turn my hand to most things, and I'm Dalton."

Finnegan flinched and then moved his horse to the side to block Dalton's path.

"I'm sure you can, Dalton."

Dalton had been working his way around a steep slope with a tangle of boulders on the summit fifty yards to his right and the moiling waters of Wilmington Creek thundering by fifty feet below him. The terrain away from the narrow trail was treacherous and if Finnegan didn't move aside Dalton wouldn't be able to ride on.

"Get out of my way," Dalton snapped, as Finnegan's attitude started to irritate.

Finnegan smiled for the first time, seemingly enjoying Dalton's more aggressive attitude.

"You're not being neighborly. Wilmington Point is a peaceable kind of town. I reckon you should turn around and head back the way you came."

Dalton nudged his jacket aside to show he was packing a gun.

"I'm going there, whether you move aside or not."

Finnegan moved in the saddle to show Dalton that he was also armed. Dalton said nothing more, forcing Finnegan to make the next move in the confrontation he was trying to set up, but his opponent remained impassive.

A minute passed. Then Finnegan flinched. A moment later scuffling sounded behind Dalton and he turned just as a rope came down over his shoulders. Dalton's sudden movement helped him to avoid having the rope loop down around his neck, but the rope was heavy and it bent him double.

The man who had sneaked up on him hurried up to his horse and then tugged. Entangled within the rope, Dalton struggled to free himself and he wavered for a moment before his assailant's insistent pulling made him slip out of the saddle.

He landed on his back with a jarring thud and lay stunned. By the time he'd shaken off his shock, his opponent had picked up the loops of rope and he used them to press down and keep him immobile.

Finnegan rode closer to loom over him. "This here is my colleague Jebediah and you picked the wrong people to mess with."

Dalton went limp and sighed, giving the impression he had surrendered. The moment Jebediah relaxed, with his back flexed against the ground, Dalton bucked his hips. Unfortunately, he had misjudged how much his fall had jarred him and he couldn't dislodge his assailant, but he did knock his hands away.

Dalton bucked again and this time as he rose up, he managed to push Jebediah away. Dalton got to his knees and thrust a leading shoulder into his assailant's stomach, making him gasp and keel over.

Then, in short order, Dalton turned the tables on Jebediah. He fought his way out from under the heavy rope and hurled it at him. The rope wrapped around Jebediah's shoulders, and when Jebediah struggled to free himself, Finnegan backed his horse away while reaching to his holster.

"You don't want to do that," Dalton said

moving for his own six-shooter.

Finnegan struggled to control his horse and that cost him valuable moments that Dalton used to draw his gun, but he didn't fire.

"We should have killed you the moment we laid eyes on you," Finnegan said with irritation.

"I wasn't aiming to cause you no trouble," Dalton said. "I just wanted to head to town and find myself some honest work."

"I don't believe you," Finnegan said, although his lowered tone didn't sound as confident as before.

Jebediah still had several coils of rope wrapped around him and he took a while to bat the rope aside, his slowness suggesting he also now thought they could have made a mistake. When he got up, he used a hand to lever himself to his feet, but his hand slipped in a patch of mud and he thudded down on his chest.

Then he went sliding off the trail. Jebediah scrambled for purchase, but he kept on slithering down the bank heading toward the creek. Dalton turned back to the other man, and Finnegan seemingly put thoughts of a confrontation from his mind as he moved his horse on toward Jebediah.

Twenty feet down the slope Jebediah managed to stop his progress, but then he panicked. His boots kicked at the dirt; his hands grasped for roots. Below him the ground became steeper and it was slick, promising him a long slide down to the churning water.

Finnegan dismounted in a hurry, but he was too late. With a cry of anguish, Jebediah's grip of the sparse vegetation came free and he slid away. Finnegan also cried out as he hurried to the edge.

Seeing that Finnegan would struggle to save his colleague, Dalton put his argument with these men from his mind and holstered his gun. He stepped up to the edge of the trail. Jebediah was sliding toward the water, and he was kicking and tearing at the earth as he searched for a handhold that would save him from landing in the water where the strong current would surely sweep him away to his death.

Dalton turned around and hurried over to the rope that had been used to attack him. With only seconds to act, he picked up as many coils as he could hold and launched them down the bank.

The rope went spiraling down to the creek passing above and then beyond Jebediah, unfurling as it dropped. Luckily, Finnegan had the presence of mind to trap one end beneath a firm boot.

Then he reached down and grabbed an equally firm grip of the rope. While Finnegan concentrated on securing his end, the other end of the rope slapped down onto the bank beyond Jebediah's form that continued to slide inexorably toward the water.

Thankfully, as Jebediah rolled past the rope, he reached for it. His first attempt missed the rope and his second attempt came loose, but on the third try his hands wrapped around a coil, albeit a foot from the end. But he still kept sliding on.

"Hold your end tightly," Dalton said, joining Finnegan in taking hold of the rope. "He's caught it."

Finnegan nodded as Jebediah slipped into the moiling water and disappeared. Then the rope moved downriver showing his progress. The rope tightened until, with a jerk, it drew up taut. The strain made both men slide forward for several feet until they dug in their heels, halting their progress.

"Start reeling him in," Finnegan said through gritted teeth. "I'll keep us anchored."

Dalton put his right hand farther down the rope and then hand over hand he drew the rope in. On the third tug, Jebediah's head broke through the water. He was gasping and kicking his legs frantically, but he was confident enough to release one hand for a moment to give an encouraging wave.

Dalton reported this to Finnegan and, with the heartening news spurring him on, he walked backward, drawing Jebediah closer to the water's edge. After a few tugs, they developed a rhythm and Dalton started to think they'd succeed, but they still had to fight for every foot as they dragged him out of the water and then up the slippery slope.

Fifty firm tugs later, they got Jebediah to the top of the bank. When they'd deposited him on safe ground, all three men sank to their knees and gathered in wheezing gasps of air. Only when they'd caught their breaths did Finnegan and Jebediah turn to Dalton. This time the truculence had gone from their eyes.

"I reckon you two have something to say to me," Dalton said.

Both men smiled before Jebediah crawled over to pat Dalton on the back.

"I reckon we do," he said. "Welcome to Wilmington Point."

* * *

Finnegan and Jebediah accompanied Dalton

to Wilmington Point, and the town turned out to be as quiet as Dalton had hoped it would be. While Finnegan rode on, Jebediah stayed with Dalton.

"You still haven't told me why you tried to bushwhack me," Dalton said.

"You saved my life so I owe you plenty," Jebediah said. "So I'll give you a warning and what you do with that information is your concern."

Dalton noted Jebediah's somber tone and he turned his horse to face him.

"Go on."

"Finnegan and me work for the bank. We were patrolling outside town because we'd heard that an infamous bank raider was heading this way. We feared you were that man and although I'm sure now that you're not him, Finnegan's gone on to the bank to warn our boss, Nugent Mix. I'm sure Nugent will want to ask you a few questions."

Dalton shrugged. "I'm no bank raider. I can answer any questions Nugent might have."

Jebediah nodded and then moved on to the bank where he directed Dalton to an office that stood at the side of the building. When they went in, Finnegan was already consulting with another man, who introduced himself as being Nugent Mix.

"You don't look like Dutch Kincaid," Nugent said. "Then again, I'm pleased my guards followed my orders and didn't take any chances."

"If Finnegan and Jebediah were only doing what you told them to do, I have no problem with them," Dalton said. "But I'd suggest you think about changing your orders. If they waylay every newcomer to town, they'll cause more trouble than they stop."

"Maybe they will, but in your case they had good cause to detain you."

Nugent moved over to a table at the side of the office and returned with a rolled-up piece of parchment, which he spread out over his desk showing that it was a Wanted poster. Dalton took his time in moving closer while trying to avoid showing his concern, but as it turned out, the poster *was* for Dutch Kincaid, a man who had a string of offenses most of which involved raids on banks.

"This man looks like plenty of trouble, but why should his crimes concern me?"

"Read the full details, Dalton."

Nugent had raised his voice when he'd stated his name and that helped Dalton to identify what had interested these men. The poster claimed that Dutch operated using several aliases, one of which was believed to be Dalton.

Dalton raised an eyebrow and nodded slowly, figuring that he ought to show a reaction. Then he read the rest of Dutch's charges, the last of which forced him to take a deep breath while he gathered his composure.

Among his numerous crimes, Dutch was wanted for killing the lawman Walker Dodge, the man who Dalton had killed. Dalton had always been prepared for the possibility that he might be blamed for misdemeanors he hadn't committed simply because he was a man with a past. He'd never considered that the same misfortune could happen to someone else and that man could find himself being blamed for Dalton's crime.

"Clearly this is an unfortunate coincidence," Dalton said. "If I ever have the pleasure of meeting this man, I'll be sure to thank him for using my name."

"My men will be sure to pass on your good wishes when they defeat him."

Dalton nodded and when Nugent pointed at the door confirming that he was now free to go, he turned to leave, but then an idea hit him. He turned back.

"With this Dutch Kincaid in the area, it sounds like you might face plenty of trouble," he said. "Do you want another guard?"

TWO

Nugent's bank reassured its customers with the proud boast that it was the safest bank in the West. To ensure he kept that promise, Nugent employed numerous guards, who worked in shifts that ensured two men were always at the bank.

Nugent took Dalton's suggestion that Finnegan and Jebediah should abandon their policy of patrolling around outside town and waylaying anyone who looked like they could be Dutch Kincaid. So when Dalton started work the next day, he joined Finnegan and Jebediah in assuming guard duties in town.

Finnegan and another guard, Giuseppe Bertello, guarded the bank in the morning, while Dalton and Jebediah patrolled around town with a roving brief to seek out trouble. Then, at noon, they would swap duties, and when the bank closed for the day, two new men would take over to guard the bank during the evening.

The level of care Nugent demanded had been effective as, aside from a few incidents over the years, he was still able to claim that his was a bank that had never been raided. As it turned out, during the morning the town was quiet and there was no sign of trouble or of Dutch having come to town, but Dalton was patient and he didn't expect a quick result.

Now that he worked for Nugent, he had put himself in a position to act if he did appear. Prior to coming to Wilmington Point, he had planned to end his troubles by killing his pursuer. He still might have to do that, but that plan wouldn't resolve the problem of why Deputy Vaughn was pursuing him in the first place.

The slice of fortune that had resulted in

Dutch being blamed for Dalton's crime provided him with a potential solution to that problem. If Dutch did what Nugent feared and came to Wilmington Point to raid the bank, Dalton would be on hand to ensure he failed.

With the number of guns Nugent had hired to deal with trouble, it was likely that Dutch would end up full of holes. Then, with Dutch's demise, Dalton's crime would be blamed permanently and officially on Dutch while Dalton would be a free man again, once he'd dealt with Deputy Vaughn.

As agreed, at noon he and Jebediah headed to the bank. While Jebediah spoke with Finnegan and they swapped tales of a quiet morning, Dalton surveyed the scene. The bank was now heaving with customers.

A queue snaked around the room, but everyone was edging forward in a good-natured manner. When Finnegan and Giuseppe moved away from their positions on either side of the door, Jebediah and Dalton moved to take over their places, but then Dalton noticed something.

Although this was his first stretch of duty, Jebediah had warned him that during the few moments while they changed guard duties, they would be distracted and this was an ideal time for someone to try something. Sure enough, a customer close to the front of the queue shoved another man making him stumble, and at the same time another man in the queue stepped aside while reaching for his holster.

"He stole that!" someone shouted.

His warning made the other three guards turn to the customers. Their orders were that in the event of trouble they should stay by the door while drawing guns on whoever was acting suspiciously, but Finnegan advanced on the man who had stepped out of the queue.

At the last moment, the man sensed him coming and he turned around, but he walked into a round-armed punch to the jaw that sent him spinning into the nearest man in the queue. That man toppled backward into another man sending him sprawling and within moments the scene became chaotic.

A lady shouted in alarm making several people scurry toward the door while someone took exception to being bumped and shoved the man who had knocked him aside, which started a fight. Worse, Finnegan had actually punched an old-timer who was cringing away and clearly not a bank raider.

That still left the first man who had acted suspiciously to be dealt with so Dalton stepped to the side so that the fleeing customers could leave the building. He failed to catch sight of this man so he caught Jebediah's eye. Jebediah shrugged and then continued to watch the bustling customers, as did Giuseppe, while Finnegan appeared to have accepted he'd punched a man who wasn't causing trouble as he was backing away.

"It's him," a customer shouted. "He's the bank raider."

The identity of the raider was unclear, but the problem appeared to resolve itself when a young man charged out from the customers. Dalton stepped forward to intercept him, but the latest cry of alarm started a new rush for the door and the mass of people blocked his way and then carried him backward. By the time he'd fought his way out of the throng and then on to the door, the young man had already slipped outside.

"Jebediah, stay here and calm things down," Dalton shouted. "I'll get him."

Dalton barged his way through the last group of customers until he emerged into clear space several paces beyond the door. The young man was hurrying away down the main drag. He gave chase, but the fleeing man was already two dozen yards ahead of him and by the time Dalton had sped up to a sprint, his quarry had increased the gap.

Then the young man darted to the right and disappeared from view behind a stable. With the feeling growing that this chase would turn out to be futile, Dalton ran on, but to his relief, when he ran around the corner of the stable, his quarry had stopped.

The young man had left a horse here, but he was clearly in a flustered state as he had yet to mount it. Dalton's arrival made him flinch and then scramble for his gun, but he was so agitated he failed to lay a hand on it at the first attempt and by then Dalton had already drawn his own gun. Dalton fired a warning shot into the ground a few feet to the side of the man making him back away quickly.

"I didn't do nothing," the man said, jerking his hand away from his holster.

"In that case, don't make this any worse on yourself," Dalton said. "Throw your gun aside and walk toward me. Make sure you move real slow and then you and I can have a quiet chat about what just happened back at the bank."

The man was ten paces away from the back of the stable and with a shrug he appeared to dismiss the thought of running away, although he still took another pace backward.

"I didn't steal nothing," he said. "I didn't get the chance."

"Like I said, we'll have a friendly chat about that, but only after you've dropped your gun on the ground."

The young man rubbed his chin nervously with a shaking hand.

"Except you won't believe me that I'm not a bank raider like that customer said. I only tried to lift a wallet out of the pocket of the man standing in front of me, but he felt me do it and he pushed me. Then everyone panicked and someone shouted out that I was trying to rob the bank."

Dalton raised his gun a mite and firmed his jaw. "I'm not listening to your excuses until you do what I said. That was your last warning."

The young man gulped. Then, with a sudden movement, he turned on his heel and sprinted for the far corner of the stable. Dalton winced, feeling unwilling to shoot the fleeing young man in the back.

He'd seen enough to accept that his quarry was so nervous he was unlikely to be a bank raider and it was more likely that he'd told the truth about being only an opportunist thief. He shouted a terse warning as he broke into a run, but the man continued to scurry away.

So he fired another warning shot into the ground, this time kicking dirt inches from the man's right foot. The young man skidded to a halt, but the gunfire hadn't stopped him. Finnegan came into view.

He walked out beyond the corner of the stable, having apparently joined in the pursuit and then taken a detour to intercept the young man from a different direction. Finnegan flinched back a pace, seemingly not having expected to come face to face with their quarry, and then threw his hand to his holster.

In response, the young man reached for his gun. This time it came to hand. Dalton had only a moment to act before the men shot at each other from a distance of only a few yards away so with a grunt of annoyance he snapped up his gun arm and fired.

His shot slammed into the young man's back before he could raise the gun. The man cried out and staggered forward a pace. He opened his mouth to say something, but the words died on his lips as he fell down to his knees.

With an almost apologetic gesture he let his gun drop back into the holster before he keeled over to lie face down in the dirt. Dalton shook his head, annoyed by this unnecessary end to the chase and then moved on. While Finnegan holstered his gun and stood back, Dalton checked on their quarry and confirmed he was dead.

"So, can Nugent still claim his bank has never been raided?" Finnegan asked.

"I reckon so," Dalton said. "This man claimed he wasn't trying to rob the bank. He was just trying to steal a wallet, and he failed to do that, too."

Finnegan chuckled. "That's not important. All that mattered is that we didn't fail."

Dalton turned the body over to lie it down on its back. Finnegan drew in his breath sharply.

"Do you recognize him?" Dalton asked.

Finnegan moved closer and stood over the body while examining the face more closely.

"I've only met him once before and that was briefly, but I remember that distinctive birthmark on the side of his neck." Finnegan pointed out the mark. "He's Wesley Tarrant, the younger brother of Rocky Tarrant, a nasty piece of work if ever there was one."

Dalton nodded. "That would suggest Wesley had already followed his brother's lead and gone bad."

"It would, but either way, Rocky isn't going to be happy when he finds out what happened to his brother." Finnegan shrugged. "So I sure am glad you're the one who shot him."

THREE

"So you're claiming that Wesley Tarrant gave you no choice but to shoot him in the back?" Sheriff Coleman said.

"If I hadn't fired, he would have killed Finnegan," Dalton said.

Coleman nodded and then headed around his desk and sat down. He leaned back in his chair and pursed his lips, suggesting that his next question would be an important one. Coleman had spent the last hour questioning the customers that had witnessed the incident in the bank.

Only then had he worked his way through the people who had been involved in trying to apprehend Wesley, and even then he'd talked with Finnegan first before he'd moved on to Dalton. As a result, Dalton had been feeling defensive before the sheriff had even asked his first question and his concern had only grown as the interview had progressed. Thankfully, Nugent had insisted on being present during the interviews and he had already given Dalton his full support.

Coleman rocked his chair forward. "How can you be so sure that this young man would have killed your associate when he didn't have the ability to carry out an act of petty pilfering without being noticed by several customers?"

"Obviously at the time I couldn't know if he would actually have the guts to fire and then whether he was a good enough shot to hit Finnegan. All I do know is that Wesley drew his gun a moment after Finnegan did, but neither of them got to fire."

"So Finnegan went for his gun first and then Wesley, but you'd already drawn your gun so you managed to shoot Wesley in the back before anyone else got the chance to fire?"

"That's what happened."

Coleman tapped his fingertips together while nodding slowly.

"According to Finnegan, he didn't go for his gun. When he saw Wesley running toward him, he only took a step backward."

Dalton thought back. Finnegan had moved for his gun. As he had been concentrating on Wesley, he hadn't seen him draw and aim, but Finnegan had holstered the gun after Wesley had been shot.

He nodded. "Finnegan did look surprised to find Wesley was so close and he did take a step backward, but then he reached for his gun."

"So now you're saying Finnegan only reached for his gun, not that he drew it."

Dalton opened his mouth and then closed it. Nugent shook his head and stepped up to the sheriff's desk.

"I'm not appreciating the direction this interview is taking," Nugent declared. "It sounds to me as if you're trying to imply something."

"I'm not implying nothing," Coleman said. "I'm just trying to understand what happened."

"It's clear what happened. Wesley tried to steal a man's wallet while he was in my bank. Due to the brave intervention of my customers and my guards, he was stopped before he could steal anything and he ran away. He was pursued and cornered, after which Dalton gave him several warnings to give himself up, but he didn't heed them."

"Then he ended up lying dead on the ground with a bullet in the back." Coleman waited until Nugent nodded and then sighed. "Do you think that when Rocky comes to town to find out what happened to his brother and I explain what happened, he'll accept without question that version of events?"

Nugent stepped back while shaking his head. "So finally, there's the reason why you're implying that my new guard acted inappropriately. Wesley is the brother of a notorious troublemaker and that means he can't be treated like just another criminal who paid the price for his crimes."

Coleman murmured an exasperated sigh. "As I told you, I'm not implying nothing. Wesley drew his gun and that gave Dalton sufficient reason to act whether Finnegan provoked Wesley into drawing or not. I just want to know why one of your guards says that he didn't draw his gun and the other one says that he did."

Nugent frowned and then turned to Dalton to provide an explanation. Now that he'd had time to think things through, Dalton reckoned he knew why there were two different versions of the incident, although he doubted the sheriff would appreciate his theory.

After Finnegan had told him who the dead man was, he had been nervous. So clearly he'd told Coleman a story that would ensure that if there were repercussions, none of the blame would land on his shoulders.

"I reacted as I saw fit," Dalton said,

settling for not inflaming the interview by making a counter-accusation. "So you should concentrate on the things we can all agree on. I gave Wesley several clear warnings. I fired two warning shots into the ground. Wesley ignored the warnings and the shots, and he drew his gun when he faced Finnegan. I shot him."

Coleman nodded. "That would appear to explain the situation, provided I can trust the man who made the claim."

Dalton stood upright and he smiled when Nugent slapped his shoulder and gave a supportive grunt.

"Dalton's only worked for me for a few hours, but I've seen already that he takes his work seriously and dutifully."

"And what did you do before then, Dalton?" Coleman asked.

Coleman raised an eyebrow. When Dalton shrugged, with a slow movement of his head the sheriff considered the Wanted posters in the corner of the room. Dalton winced and then covered his concern by spreading his hands.

"If you're talking about the poster of Dutch Kincaid that also happens to have my name on it, I can assure you that man isn't me."

Coleman smiled. "Of course you can assure me of that. The man looks nothing like you."

The three men stood in silence until Nugent edged forward.

"Does that conclude this interview to your satisfaction?" he said.

"It's answered my questions," Coleman said. "It's yet to be seen whether Rocky accepts that his brother was at fault."

Dalton acknowledged this was unlikely with a frown. Then he turned away and headed to the door. Nugent joined him and the two men remained silent as they headed along the main drag.

When they reached the bank, Nugent signified that Dalton should join him in his office. Dalton noted that this would delay him seeing Finnegan for a while, which was probably sensible as Dalton doubted he'd be able to keep his cool. Nugent closed the door behind him and faced him.

"So did Finnegan draw his gun, or do you only think you saw him draw it?" he asked.

"I saw Finnegan's hand move to his holster as did Wesley, but I'll admit I can't say for certain what happened next as I then concentrated on dealing with Wesley. Either way, Finnegan should have admitted he made that move."

"Except he didn't so, assuming that he doesn't change his story, will you and he be able to work with each other again after this?"

Dalton snorted. "I'll be able to work with him, but he might have some problems after I've broken his jaw."

Nugent laughed, but then provided a serious expression.

"Then we have a problem. I can't have personal animosity distracting my guards from carrying out their duties, and you've worked for me for six hours while Finnegan has been with me for six months."

Dalton raised his chin. "If that's your decision, I won't ask you to reconsider. I just hope you never have to rely on Finnegan, as clearly he'll help himself first and anyone else second."

"I agree, but I don't ask much from the men that guard my bank other than that they guard my bank." Nugent smiled. "It would appear from recent events that you have abilities that are more useful to me than just that limited role."

Dalton narrowed his eyes. "What are you saying?"

"I'm saying I have a new job for you, and it's one I can give only to you." Nugent headed behind his desk and sat down. "I've given up on my plan to stop Dutch reaching town, but then again I'm not enjoying the alternate plan of waiting for him to arrive. So I want you to find him."

The offer made Dalton raise a surprised eyebrow. "Do you have any clues about where he might be?"

"After Finnegan and Jebediah made a mistake in waylaying you yesterday, I've been asking around. The rumor is that he has been seen lurking around Lerado. Apparently, he's bringing together a gang to raid my bank. I want you to find him, become a member of that gang and, when you've learned his plans, pass that information on to me so I can stop him."

Dalton tipped back his hat. "I'm intrigued by the offer and I'm honored that you think I could do it, but I'll be honest with you. I've never done anything like that before."

"That's not as important as the fact that you're in an ideal position to infiltrate Dutch's gang and bring them down. We'll know the truth about our agreement, but as far as everyone else is concerned, you no longer work for me after you overreacted to a situation and gunned down a man. Then there's the rumor that your name is on a Wanted poster."

Dalton nodded. "So by a mixture of coincidence and ill-fortune I've been handed a plausible cover story that I'm a disgruntled man who used to work for you. A man like that would hate you and he'd be sure to have information that could be useful to a bank raider."

"That's what I figure, but it'll be a tough assignment. When you find Dutch, you may have to ride with him for a while."

Nugent stood up and leaned over the desk with his hand held out. Dalton rubbed his chin and then took the hand.

"I understand," he said.

Nugent smiled. "And, of course, you shouldn't forget that there's a bounty of five thousand dollars on Dutch's head. If you bring him in, that bounty is yours."

FOUR

"Is it true?" Jebediah asked when Dalton joined him at the bar in the Lone Star saloon that evening.

"It is," Dalton said. "It seems you'll be getting a new partner."

Jebediah poured Dalton a large whiskey. "I'd only had my new partner for a day, but I had no problem with him."

"It's good to hear that, but I don't reckon many others will see it that way."

Jebediah frowned. "I feared the worst when I heard Finnegan telling everyone you got trigger-happy and gunned down Rocky Tarrant's brother even though he'd stolen nothing."

"I guess that sums up what happened."

Dalton took a gulp of his drink. "Provided you ignore the bit where I saved Finnegan's life."

"It sounds as if that was your only mistake."

Dalton laughed and then adopted a serious expression as he leaned on the bar beside Jebediah.

"I reckon it was. I was sure that Wesley would be so spooked when he saw Finnegan going for his gun that he would defend himself, and when I think back about it, I still think that."

"Then Nugent should have sided with you," Jebediah snapped, waving an arm angrily. "I'm sure not going to work for a man who—"

Dalton raised a hand silencing Jebediah. "Don't go saying something that'll get you looking for a new job, too."

Jebediah shook his head. "I'm not sure I want that job if it means having to accept the word of men like Finnegan."

Dalton swirled his drink as he thought

about what he should say to calm Jebediah down. He had known Nugent's mission would be tough when he'd accepted it, as it would call for him to lie convincingly.

Already he wanted to tell Jebediah the truth so that he wouldn't escalate the situation. Worse, Jebediah trusted him, but the people he would encounter later would have no reason to believe him.

"Finnegan's version of events is a matter between me and him," he said, settling for the policy of saying little.

This response appeared to work as Jebediah nodded, making Dalton sigh with relief. Then they talked about what Dalton would do next, which gave him the opportunity to explain the story he'd decided beforehand that he'd go back west, as this direction would let him visit Lerado where Dutch had been seen recently.

An hour later, Jebediah was more content, but he tensed up when Finnegan and Giuseppe arrived in the saloon. Despite Dalton's decision not to talk about today's

43

events, he didn't want to leave town without confronting Finnegan, no matter what effect it had on his cover story.

He turned around to lean back against the bar. Several customers broke off from their conversation, confirming that word had spread about the incident, and in a saloon room that was growing quieter with every passing moment, Finnegan walked inside.

He stopped two paces from Dalton while Giuseppe moved on to stand beside Jebediah at the bar, his action presumably showing that he didn't want to get involved in their disagreement.

"I hear you no longer work for the bank," Finnegan said, his voice loud enough to ensure everyone in the saloon heard him.

"I gather that Nugent always puts the welfare of his customers first," Dalton said, equally loudly. "It would have been hard for him to keep me on at the bank after what happened today."

"I agree. He trusts his guards to keep his customers safe." Finnegan licked his lips.

"Nobody can trust a man who shoots someone in the back."

Several customers drew in their breath sharply and the comment made the last of the conversation in the saloon die out.

"They wouldn't, if that is what had happened." Dalton took a pace forward to stand up to Finnegan. "Except you and me were there, and we both know there's more to that tale than just its sorry outcome."

"Wesley Tarrant tried to steal a wallet while he was in the bank and then he ran away, so I guess you're right that he doesn't deserve no sympathy."

"I didn't mean that. You chased after Wesley, too, and you surprised him so much he went for his gun."

"I did give chase, but I tried to calm the situation down by raising my hands and backing away." Finnegan carried out that action, clearly making the point that earlier today he'd acted reasonably and he was doing the same here. "I reckon I could have talked him down, but we'll never know that now."

"That's an interesting version of events. To me, it looked as if you went for your gun and when Wesley responded in kind, I shot him before he could kill you."

Finnegan raised a hand and flexed his fingers. Then he mimed shooting rapidly around the saloon room.

"Everyone knows I'm a quick and accurate shot, and I could see that Wesley was a frightened kid who couldn't keep his hand steady for long enough to pilfer a wallet. If I'd drawn first, Wesley would never have had the time to reach his gun, never mind shoot me."

"You make a good point, but you're ignoring one matter. I'm saying I saw you reach for your gun and that's what made Wesley draw, which means you're lying."

Finnegan jutted his jaw, as if thinking about his reply. Then, with a backhanded swipe, he struck out. Dalton had anticipated Finnegan's action and while jerking his head away he thrust up an arm, blocking the blow before the fist hit his cheek.

Dalton followed through with a short-armed jab into Finnegan's side that made his opponent grunt before he bundled Finnegan away. Finnegan stumbled back for a few paces until he barged into two customers standing at the bar.

These men righted him and pushed him back. Within moments the customers closed in to form a circle around them. Dalton was pleased to note that although Finnegan was well-known in town, their murmurs of encouragement were evenly directed at both of them.

Dalton stood his ground, making Finnegan come to him so that everyone would see that he was acting more aggressively, and Finnegan duly obliged. He stormed forward and with his fists whirling, he threw rapid punches at Dalton's head and chest.

As before, Dalton blocked the first blow and then the next one, but Finnegan was relentless and the third blow caught the point of his chin knocking his head aside. Then Finnegan followed through with a kick to Dalton's shin that made him hobble back for a pace and then a swiping blow to the cheek upended him.

This time it was Dalton's turn to go stumbling into the watching customers. When they pushed him away, he used his momentum to launch a scything blow into Finnegan's stomach that made him fold over.

Then he slapped both hands on Finnegan's back and ran him forward before releasing him. Finnegan ran on and he was moving quickly enough to break through the circle of customers and go crashing into a table.

Dalton rolled his shoulders as he waited for Finnegan's return. Finnegan didn't keep him waiting for long. He came storming out from the milling customers with his head still down and thudded into Dalton's stomach with a leading shoulder.

He pushed Dalton on until Dalton's feet

slid out from under him and the two men went crashing down on the floor. Then, with their limbs entangled, the fighting became frantic with both men hurling wild blows and kicks at each other.

They rolled over each other and across the floor, knocking them into other people's legs as they struggled to gain an advantage. Dalton delivered more punches than he received and he reckoned he was getting the upper hand, but then their scrambling progress across the floor made them fetch up against a wall.

Finnegan took advantage of the situation by grabbing Dalton's jaw and slamming his head back against the wall. Dalton heard a dull thud that reverberated through his head and neck, and when Finnegan slammed his head back a second time, the thud wasn't so loud, giving him the impression his head might have softened the wall.

The next he knew Finnegan was dragging him to his feet and his vision was swirling. He stumbled to the side, his legs feeling so numb they wouldn't support him, and he found it even harder to stand upright when Finnegan launched a round-armed punch to his jaw that sent him reeling across the saloon room.

Dalton hit a table and doubled up over it, after which Finnegan dragged him upright and punched him in the opposite direction. This time there was no table to stop him and he staggered backward and then toppled over.

He lay on his back, groaning and feeling too weak to stop Finnegan hitting him again. Thankfully, Finnegan only stood over him.

"As everyone can see, I'm a man who ends fights, not starts them," Finnegan declared. "You're a man who can only win fights where he can shoot men in the back."

Dalton couldn't muster the energy to retort, but when Jebediah started remonstrating with Finnegan he forced himself to get to his knees. Then he stood up, although the movement made him feel faint and he staggered for an uncertain pace before he got himself under control.

"I saved your life today, Finnegan," he called, making Finnegan turn away from Jebediah to face him. "If you're so scared about what Rocky Tarrant will do that you're not prepared to thank me, that's not my problem."

Finnegan snarled, his anger making his eyes wide and glaring proving that no matter whose version of events was the more accurate, he had spoken the truth. Dalton got another punch to the jaw for his trouble that toppled him backward.

Then Finnegan dragged him to his feet and ran him at the door. Dalton hit the batwings with a leading shoulder, fell down to his knees on the boardwalk and then rolled over to lie on his back on the hardpan.

"If I ever see your face in this saloon again, you'll get the same treatment," Finnegan shouted over the batwings.

Dalton's only reply was a groan so Finnegan taunted him some more, but the bustle in the saloon started up again and Finnegan headed back to the bar. Presently, an argument flared inside as Jebediah remonstrated with someone. Then Jebediah came bustling outside while sporting a thunderous expression and kneeled beside him.

"You may have lost that fight, but Finnegan won't get the last word," he said. "I'll make sure of that."

"I'm obliged," Dalton said. He got to his knees and prodded his various sore spots. "Either way, I reckon it's time I moved on, so that's one battle I don't need to have again just yet."

Jebediah smiled. "Does that mean that one day you'll come back this way?"

"One day I will," Dalton said. "Depending on how things go, when I do return, I reckon I might need the support of a good friend again."

FIVE

Dalton decided that to get close to Dutch he needed to start with the source of the rumor Nugent had heard about Dutch's recent movements, which was Kendrew McKay. Kendrew lived in Lerado, which was two days' riding from Wilmington Point, although Nugent had told him that Kendrew only passed on information and he wouldn't help him in any other way.

Dalton rode out of Wilmington Point without seeing either Finnegan or Jebediah again. When he arrived in Lerado late in the day, he soon confirmed that he wouldn't get any easy answers. Kendrew looked after the town's stable and while he took Dalton's horse into a stall Dalton reported to him that he knew Nugent, but Kendrew reacted with only a shrug.

"Nugent's a popular man," Kendrew said with a level tone while not meeting his eye. "He knows plenty of people."

"He does, and he's a man who likes to avoid trouble, as do I," Dalton said. "So I hope Lerado is a safe place to stay for the night."

"It's not, so the only advice I can offer you is not to invite trouble. Keep to yourself and don't talk to nobody that you don't have to."

Dalton noted the hint that Kendrew wouldn't provide him with useful information. So he rubbed his jaw as he sought a way to probe in a way that wouldn't put Kendrew in danger from the men he wanted to find.

"Is there anyone in particular I should avoid?" he asked.

"Everyone but me."

Kendrew laughed and then walked away. Dalton accepted that attitude, for now, and moved on to the First Chance, the town's only saloon, which turned out to be as unpromising a source of information as he had feared.

Although it was early evening, only two other customers were within and they paid no attention to him, while the bartender, Enoch, showed no interest in Dalton's story that he was just passing through. When he had a mug of coffee, Dalton sat at a table by the window and thought about his options.

Lerado comprised around a dozen buildings and aside from Kendrew and the men in the saloon, he'd seen nobody else here. He decided to be patient and accept that the lack of people was a promising sign as it suggested everyone else was together somewhere, but the night wore on without anyone else appearing.

When even the two customers sloped off into the night, he accepted that he wouldn't make progress tonight in finding anyone who knew how he could find Dutch. So he asked Enoch about getting a room for the night.

Thankfully, he had one available at the back of the saloon so Dalton rested up and put his hopes in finding a source of useful information tomorrow. As it turned out, the next morning proved to be as quiet as his first day in town had been so after eating in the saloon, Dalton headed to the same table as yesterday where he ordered coffee.

"I thought you intended to move on," Enoch said.

"I had intended to do that, but now that I've seen Lerado, I reckon I might stay for a while."

Enoch shrugged. "Custom is always welcome, but nothing ever happens here."

"I know," Dalton said.

When Enoch smiled and then left, Dalton settled down in his chair and waited. Before long, his policy of not pressing for information appeared to work as when the first customer arrived, he and Enoch exchanged quiet words.

Dalton was now becoming more adept at overhearing quiet conversation and he learned that the customer was called Lief, while a second customer, who arrived shortly afterward, was Willoughby. This man repeated Lief's subtle consideration of him and Dalton wasn't surprised when Willoughby came over to his table.

"So you're planning on sitting around in this saloon drinking coffee for a while, are you?" he said.

"I thought I would," Dalton said using a neutral tone.

"Men who stay here are either looking for someone, or looking to avoid someone. Which one are you?"

"I'm just someone who likes the quiet." Dalton smiled. "Which type are you?"

"I'm the type who avoids people who look like trouble."

Willoughby returned the smile and headed to the bar. Dalton figured that subtle warning meant the townsfolk were now starting to accept he was a man with a private mission. His hopes were raised further when in early afternoon five riders trotted into town.

Willoughby headed outside to greet them and a brief debate ensued. Then the group moved off, leaving Willoughby to help Kendrew take their horses to the stable. When the men had disappeared from view, Lief and Enoch both frowned, so Dalton took his mug to the bar.

"It's good to see more people in town," Dalton said in a conversational manner.

"I'm surprised that a man who likes the quiet would enjoy seeing them," Enoch said as he filled his mug.

"A man can have too much quiet," Dalton said and then moved on to the door.

As there were few places where the newcomers could have gone, he figured they had probably headed into a derelict building on the edge of town. He also figured Enoch's guarded comment meant these men were troublesome, which meant they could be connected to Dutch, or might even include him.

Dalton supped his drink. Then, figuring

this was the right time for him to take more chances, he slipped outside and moseyed up and down the main drag. He adopted a casual demeanor, but he confirmed the building on the edge of town had once been another saloon when the town had enjoyed better days.

Men were moving around inside so he headed back to the stable where he leaned back against the wall in a position that kept both saloons in sight. Presently, Willoughby came outside and with a sly smile on his face he joined Dalton and mimicked his posture.

"Did you see anything interesting?" Willoughby asked.

"Nope," Dalton said.

"Then I reckon it's time for you to move on."

Dalton shrugged. "I'm in no hurry."

"Maybe you're not, but you didn't listen to me earlier. I avoid people who look like trouble, and you're showing too much interest in what's going on around town for my liking."

"You can't blame a man for showing an interest. I'm down to my last few dollars and I'm getting to think I ought to find a way to change that."

"Nobody here can help you with that. So leave."

Willoughby pushed away from the wall and strode away. A few moments later the door of the derelict saloon opened and someone stood in the doorway. Willoughby raised a hand briefly and then stopped and turned to Dalton.

Dalton figured he'd now done what he'd set out to do and gathered the interest of people who might be able to help him, and that left him with the problem of how to use the opportunity. He smiled and then tipped his hat to Willoughby before heading into the stable.

Nugent's informant, Kendrew, was loitering in the shadows and he came over without meeting his eye. Dalton checked that Willoughby was still pacing around outside, presumably to ensure he left, and then moved into a position where he was just out of his sight. Then he withdrew a few dollars from his inside pocket and held them out.

"I'm leaving," Dalton said.

Kendrew nodded. "I reckon that's sensible, but that's more generous than you need to be."

"It is, but take the money, anyhow."

Kendrew's fingers edged toward the bills and then moved back.

"Why would a man who's been told to leave town want to pay three times more than he needs to?"

"Because I want something from you."

"I've already told you. I can't help you. I don't know nothing about nothing."

"I'd already accepted that, but I just want you to take the money." Dalton winked. "Then I want you to starting yelling for help."

SIX

With his brow furrowed, Kendrew took the offered money. Then, with a shrug, he yelped. The sound was the kind Dalton would expect someone who had stubbed their toe to make rather than someone who was in mortal danger, but it had the desired effect.

A shadow moved beyond the doorway as Willoughby came closer. So Dalton snatched the money back from Kendrew and then barged him aside, this action making Kendrew screech in a more convincing manner.

Dalton turned away with the money held high, just in case Willoughby hadn't seen what he'd done and moved off toward his horse. He walked slowly to ensure Willoughby would have enough time to remonstrate with him, but as it turned out Willoughby hurried off.

So Dalton collected his horse and by the time he led it outside Willoughby had gathered the townsfolk outside and they'd formed a loose arc to block his path. Annoyingly, Enoch and Lief were at the front while the newcomers loitered behind them.

"You're not leaving town," Enoch said.

"First I was told to leave, now I'm told to stay," Dalton said.

"That was before you stole money off Kendrew."

Dalton patted his pocket. "I didn't steal nothing. That was my money and I took it back because I didn't like the hospitality here."

Kendrew sloped through the stable doorway, his eyes downcast as he showed his displeasure in being dragged into Dalton's ruse. Then, with a shrug, Enoch appeared to accept the inevitable.

"Apparently, this man used to work for

Nugent Mix," he said quickly, as if by speaking rapidly he might reduce everyone's interest in his presence. "He lost his job, so I guess he thought he needed his money more than I do."

Dalton hadn't told Kendrew, or anyone else in Lerado, his cover story, figuring he would use it only when it could be effective and it was likely to be believed. While Dalton was wondering how Kendrew knew about his past when news about the events in Wilmington Point didn't appear to have reached Lerado, Willoughby stepped forward to join Enoch.

"I knew you had a reason for coming here," he said. "You're trouble and we don't need trouble."

Dalton's ruse hinged on someone working out that he could be of use to Dutch, which would encourage that person to step in and stop the developing confrontation. Unfortunately, everybody just sneered at him with the antipathy he'd expect townsfolk to show to men who tried to leave town without paying.

He figured that he might have been wrong and that the newcomers weren't connected to Dutch, so he walked on, but that encouraged Willoughby and the others to move in on him. Willoughby grabbed his shoulder, halting him while Enoch and Lief stood before him. This encouraged Kendrew to move closer, but that was only to take the reins of his horse and then lead it away.

"I guess I don't need my money that badly," Dalton said reaching to his pocket. "Take it."

Enoch moved in and knocked Dalton's hand away before it touched his pocket while in a coordinated move Willoughby tipped Dalton's gun from its holster. Dalton pushed Enoch away and then turned to confront Willoughby, but Lief grabbed him a bear hug from behind trapping his arms against his side.

Willoughby then wasted no time in punching Dalton in the stomach, and when that made him fold over, he slapped his cheek backhanded making him stand up straight again. Then Willoughby riffled through his pockets, claiming the money he had apparently refused to give Kendrew.

"So you annoyed Nugent, did you?" Willoughby said as he waved the money above his head.

"So they say," Dalton said as Kendrew took the money. "Then again, they say plenty of things about me."

"I'd guess they do, so I reckon we should do what Nugent did and get rid of you."

Dalton reckoned this was his best moment to state his case, even though he still didn't know if anyone who might lead him to Dutch was around to hear it.

"One day soon I intend to make Nugent regret the day he crossed me," he snarled. "So don't make the same mistake he did."

"You just earned yourself a beating," Willoughby said and then launched a scything blow to Dalton's cheek that almost tore him away from Lief's firm grip.

Dalton shook off the blow while Kendrew

narrowed his eyes, suggesting he wouldn't help him. Accordingly, Kendrew folded his arms when Willoughby thumped Dalton in the stomach and he shook his head when Willoughby stepped aside for Enoch to deliver a sharp uppercut to his chin that turned him around.

This position at least let Dalton face the line of men who hadn't gotten involved in the skirmish, but they stood impassively with no suggestion that his past interested them. Dalton figured he needed to abandon all thoughts of trying to impress them and instead he went limp.

The action didn't catch Lief by surprise. He continued to hold him with a tight grip while Willoughby and Enoch again lined up to take their turn in thumping him. Dalton made no effort to avoid their blows and he received another two punches to the chest.

Any hope that his assailants might now relent fled when they muttered with derision about his apparent resilience and then moved in to hit him again. Fortunately, Lief appeared to accept Dalton's pretense of being too weak to fight them off, as his movements were unhurried when he loosened his hold of Dalton's chest and then moved to grasp his arms.

The moment Lief's hands touched his upper arms Dalton dropped to one knee, evading Lief's attempted lunge. Then he scrambled forward out of Lief's reach before coming up quickly.

Willoughby and Enoch both lurched forward to grab him, so Dalton twisted to the side and when he found that open ground was ahead of him he ran. He managed three scrambling paces before one of his assailants grabbed him from behind making him stumble.

In a berserk action he threw off his attacker, but received a glancing blow in return from another man that sent him tumbling. He rolled over twice and came up on his feet, and then tried again to hurry on.

This time, he found he was running toward the quiet group from the derelict saloon. He didn't vary his route and with smirks on their faces the men parted to let him run through their midst.

With clear ground ahead Dalton ran on, but when he'd covered a dozen paces and a pursuit had failed to get underway, he stopped. Dalton presumed that as he'd have to come back to claim his horse, his three tormentors were waiting to find out what his next move would be. Then another man came out of the derelict saloon.

"So what are you going to do now?" the man called.

"I've been wrongly accused, again," Dalton said. "So I'll be getting my property back."

The man smiled. "I'll be interested to see how you do that. The townsfolk appear determined to take out their anger on someone."

Lief and the others had bunched up, although they were making no move to escalate the situation. With a nod to himself Dalton decided that their lack of action had more to do with the newcomer than himself.

"This town has been acting mighty strange since I arrived," he said. "Before I leave I reckon I'm just riled up enough now to take out my irritation on someone."

Dalton tipped his hat and took determined paces toward the group. He walked past the building, but then to his relief the man spoke up.

"I can see that you're riled," he said. "So before you deal with them, I'd like to hear more about why you no longer work for Nugent."

Dalton was glad that he was facing away so that the man couldn't see his relieved expression now that he'd finally found someone who could be involved with the men he wanted.

"What's it to you?" he said, turning back.

"I'm Dutch Kincaid. You may have heard of me."

Dalton nodded. Then he tipped back his hat to give him a moment to think about the right way to respond. He decided that revealing as little of his cover story as possible along with some honesty would serve him best.

"I have a score to settle with Nugent, so I came here looking for the man who concerns him the most, but I'd started to think I'd made a mistake."

"I'm pleased to hear he's concerned about me."

Dutch raised an eyebrow, presumably requesting his name. As he had decided to keep the lies to a minimum, Dalton provided it. Dutch's only reaction was a brief nod, suggesting that the alias displayed on his Wanted poster was a mistake that must have been made when Dutch had been blamed for Dalton's crime.

Then Dutch gestured for Dalton to join him in the saloon before moving inside. Behind him, the men who had been watching the altercation advanced while his tormentors sloped off, confirming who among them were the townsfolk and who were with Dutch.

Dalton moved on and when he slipped

inside, Dutch was already leaning back against the bar. Only one other man was inside and he ignored Dalton. So, while the others filed in after him, Dalton moved forward to stand in the center of the room.

"Nugent sure is concerned that you're planning to raid his bank," Dalton said. "When I worked for him I was determined to stop you, but now I like the thought of Nugent getting that smug grin wiped off his face."

Dutch rubbed his jaw while regarding him. "If you'd have come here offering your services a few days ago, I'd have let the townsfolk run you out of town, but now sadly I find I'm need of information."

"Why?"

Dutch turned to the other man at the bar, and this man stepped forward, his narrowed eyes and firm-set jaw giving Dalton a hint of what he might say before he spoke.

"Because my brother, Wesley Tarrant, was supposed to find out about the bank," the man said. "Then someone shot him."

SEVEN

"I'd heard about a young man getting shot," Dalton said levelly, facing up to Rocky. "Your brother died on the day I lost my job."

"Then you already know more than I do," Rocky said. He raised an eyebrow in a request for Dalton to explain further.

Dalton moved on to the bar to cover up his relief now that it sounded as if Rocky didn't know that he was with the man who had shot Wesley.

"I was patrolling around town at the time looking out for trouble, but I gather your brother was acting suspiciously while he was in the bank and he tried to steal from a customer. A bank guard chased him outside and he got gunned down."

Rocky winced. "I should never have trusted Wesley with that job. I told him to find out what sort of protection Nugent had at the bank and he must have gotten it into his head to steal so he'd draw out the guards."

"If that was his plan, he picked the wrong place to try it."

"I'm obliged for the information." Rocky shrugged. "So why did Nugent get rid of you?"

"Nugent not only had men patrolling in the bank and around town, but out of town waylaying people who were heading for Wilmington Point. So when a young man was shot for petty pilfering, it proved that Nugent was overreacting. He accepted the criticism and reduced the number of guns. I was the last man he hired, so I was the first one he fired."

Dutch gave a brief nod, so Rocky turned back to the bar.

"Then you can be helpful to us, and more importantly, you can be helpful to me. When we get to Wilmington Point, you'll show me the guard who gunned down my brother."

Dalton thought for a moment. He figured that while he was trying to win Dutch's confidence, a vague answer would weaken his cover story, and he owed Finnegan no favors after the way he'd behaved after the gunfight.

"The man you want is a lying, cheating, double-crossing varmint by the name of Finnegan O'Doyle. It'll be my pleasure to pick him out for you."

Rocky grunted his approval and then leaned back against the bar while Dutch signified that Dalton should join him at a corner table. The rest of the men collected chairs and gathered around.

Nobody questioned Dutch's decision to accept him into the group, affirming the impression Nugent had provided that Dutch was a leader who controlled every aspect of his criminal endeavors.

"This man is the latest and final member of our team," Dutch declared when his group of rough-clad and cold-eyed men had settled down. "He's going to tell us every-thing we want to know about Wilmington Point, its bank and its protection. Then we'll finalize our plans."

A few men muttered comments that cast doubt on Dalton's ability to be helpful while sneering at him.

"I can tell you plenty about the bank," Dalton said, raising his voice to address everyone with assurance. "It should be enough to help you complete your mission."

"That's good," Dutch said, as Dalton's comment stilled the discontent and even gathered a few murmured supportive comments from the group.

Dalton spread his hands. "But I have to admit that I wasn't in Wilmington Point for long so I might not be able to tell you much about the town other than to show you its layout."

"I can accept that," Dutch smiled, but then leaned forward and narrowed his eyes. "What I can't accept is deception. If you give me any cause to doubt you, you'll be dead before you get a chance to explain yourself."

* * *

The group of twelve men left for Wilmington Point in the morning, the rest of Dutch's team having joined Dutch the previous night. They rode swiftly, but Dutch directed them on a circuitous route that ensured they would approach the town going upriver, which lengthened the journey to a three-day ride.

Everyone rode quietly in a tight formation and despite Dutch's stern warning Dalton didn't detect that Dutch's men eyed him with suspicion any longer. He presumed that everyone else had received the same warning, and last night he had been open and useful in providing the information Dutch had requested.

He had drawn a map of the town and detailed the patrol route that he and Jebediah had followed, along with the patrols that he knew had been carried out outside town. Then he'd drawn the layout of the bank noting the positions of the guards along with their routine.

All this was based on his short day working for Nugent, but the information had appeared to satisfy Dutch. With his acceptance, Dalton had then mingled freely with the group and he'd not seen the townsfolk again.

That night they camped out on open ground. Dutch posted guards and none of the gang strayed outside of the camp. Although they encountered no trouble, for the next two days they continued with this policy of being cautious and staying together.

On the third night, they settled down an hour's riding away from Wilmington Point. With everyone again staying close together, Dalton put his mind to how he could pass on the information he had learned to Nugent.

His instructions had been to ride with Dutch until he'd learned his plans and then relay those details, but with Dutch keeping a tight rein on the group that wouldn't be easy. If he tried to sneak away, someone would surely notice him, so he thought about various explanations for why he should leave the group for a while.

As he couldn't come up with a reason for leaving that he reckoned Dutch would accept, he had resigned himself to taking the risk of slipping away in the night when Dutch gathered everyone's attention. Then he detailed the full plan for tomorrow.

The raid would take place in early afternoon using Wesley's ill-fated plan of acting while the guards changed duties. To prepare for this raid, throughout the morning everyone would slip into town in pairs.

Dutch allocated who those groups would be and he paired Dalton up with Rocky, who nodded as if he'd been expecting that. Dutch then detailed the pretexts that everyone would use for being in town, including various innocent sounding excuses such as looking for work or needing supplies.

Dutch gave Dalton permission to show Rocky where his brother had died, and although this was an obvious reason for his being in town, Rocky muttered angrily to himself. Then he stormed away from the campfire.

Dutch hurried after him and a brief, heated conversation ensued ending with both men returning to the fire. Rocky sat hunched over and Dutch made no reference to what had just transpired.

Instead, he finished his instructions by covering the actual raid, which he would lead with Buster Lackey, the man who had been with him the longest. Then everyone settled down for the night and, as Dalton figured that finding a reason to sneak away from one man tomorrow would be easier than getting away from eleven men tonight, he resolved to bide his time.

In the morning, the raiders moved on together. When they'd halved the distance to town, the six pairs parted and set about heading on to Wilmington Point using the various routes Dutch had specified. Dalton and Rocky would be the last pair to arrive before Dutch and Buster rode into town to start the raid, as both men might be recognized and this would limit the time during which something unexpected could happen.

"This will be tough on you," Dalton said when he caught his first sight of the town. "It's a pity we couldn't have got here quicker to give you more time."

Rocky nodded. "Dutch figured that seeing where Wesley got gunned down would put me in the right frame of mind for the raid."

"I'd guess that's what you got annoyed about last night."

"You guessed right. Somehow, I can't feel enthused about what's going to happen today anymore." Rocky shrugged. "I assume that's why he paired you up with me, to make sure I'll go through with the raid."

Dalton chuckled. "There was me wondering whether he'd paired you up with me to make sure I went through with it. I joined the group last and I've got the impression Dutch doesn't trust me completely."

"Dutch doesn't trust anybody completely. That's why he's been so successful."

With this exchange giving Dalton some hope that he might be able to find a reason to leave the depressed Rocky alone for long enough to pass information on to Nugent, they moved on. When they arrived in town, they rode past the bank and two of the pairs of raiders that were out on the main drag. Then they moved on to the stable where they dismounted at the side.

"This is where it happened," Dalton said, gesturing vaguely ahead even though he knew the exact spot where Wesley had been standing when he'd shot him.

"Tell me what you know," Rocky said.

"I don't know much beyond the fact that Wesley ran from the bank to the stable, presumably to get to his horse, but he didn't reach it."

"That's because of Finnegan O'Doyle?"

Dalton didn't trust himself to do anything

other than nod, but Rocky was too busy surveying the scene to notice his concern at the lies he was telling. When Rocky shuffled forward while examining the ground, Dalton turned to the main drag and found that they had been noticed.

Jebediah and Giuseppe were standing at the corner of the stable watching Rocky with interest. Then Jebediah moved toward them, but Dalton caught his eye and shooed him away before pointing at the front of the stable.

Jebediah got his meaning and veered away, but when Dalton turned back, Rocky was frowning, suggesting he had seen him make the gestures, although he probably hadn't noticed that he'd made the gestures to one of the guards.

"I reckon Wesley came running from the corner of the stable," Dalton said. "He nearly reached the far end over there."

Dalton pointed behind him and then ahead making Rocky nod, seemingly accepting that explanation as being the reason why he had been gesturing.

"Over there?" he asked moving to where Dalton had indicated.

"I reckon." Dalton smiled. "You take all the time you need. I'll check that nobody's paying us any attention."

He didn't wait for Rocky to agree to separate and he moved off, although when he reached the corner of the stable he stopped. Rocky had his back to him and he was shuffling around as he appraised the scene.

Dalton slipped around the corner. Giuseppe was standing some distance away, but Jebediah was waiting for him. It was likely that some of the raiders would be watching him, but he figured that checking out if they were would look more suspicious than talking openly.

"I never expected to see you with Rocky Tarrant," Jebediah said with his eyebrows raised. "Have you—?"

"He doesn't know what happened here and I haven't made my peace with him,"

Dalton said, speaking quickly. "That's of n consequence right now. I have something important to tell you, so don't ask no questions and just listen."

Jebediah straightened up. "I'm listening."

"I couldn't tell anyone, but Nugent tasked me with infiltrating Dutch Kincaid's gang and foiling his plans. I'm currently doing just that. Dutch is aiming to raid the bank within the hour. I can't get away from Rocky without alerting the raiders who are lurking around town, so you need to tell Nugent."

Jebediah's eyes opened wide before with a shake of the shoulders he got his surprise under control.

"I'll do that." Jebediah smiled, looking as if he wanted to continue talking and learn more, but when Dalton backed away for a short pace, with a quick nod he appeared to accept the urgency of the situation. "Be careful, Dalton."

With that, he turned away and then signified to Giuseppe that they should walk on. They walked away without undue haste giving the impression they were just resuming their patrol.

When they moved to cross over the main drag toward the bank, Dalton turned around, and then flinched when he found that Rocky had been standing behind him. Rocky frowned and then slipped back around the corner.

Dalton didn't know whether Rocky had heard his brief conversation with Jebediah, but he figured he probably hadn't had enough time to hear anything that might cause him trouble. So he put on a calm expression and followed him around the corner only to come to a sudden halt when he found himself looking down the barrel of a gun.

"Dutch told us not to speak to anyone," Rocky said. He firmed his gun hand to sight Dalton's forehead. "So what were you saying to that man?"

"Jebediah is a bank guard and I knew him from when I was last in town," Dalton said with a placating smile. "Not speaking to him would have looked more suspicious than acknowledging him."

"I can accept that, but it sounded to me as if you were telling Jebediah to warn Nugent about the raid."

"I guess it might have sounded like that."

Rocky narrowed his eyes. Then he nodded and lowered his gun.

"That's good," he said. "It'll save me having to warn him."

EIGHT

"You're working for Nugent, too?" Dalton said with surprise.

"No, but I sure as hell don't want Dutch's raid to succeed," Rocky said.

"Because of what happened to your brother?"

Rocky nodded and then checked that nobody was close by. Then both men walked slowly away from the corner.

"I owed an old debt to Dutch and last month he called it in by asking for my help to raid the bank. I've got a bad reputation here, so I recruited my brother to check out the situation. After what happened to Wesley, my only aim now is to find the guard who killed him and to make sure

Dutch doesn't profit from his death."

Rocky raised an eyebrow requesting Dalton's explanation for his actions. Dalton pondered for a moment and he decided that after Rocky's revelation, the truth would serve him better than any alternate explanation.

"After your brother died, Nugent reckoned he needed to find a way to stop Dutch that didn't involve hiring a whole heap of guns. So he sent me to find Dutch, infiltrate his gang and stop him."

Rocky whistled under his breath. "He must be paying you plenty for a mission as dangerous as that."

"He's not. There's a bounty on Dutch's head and if I can bring him down, it's mine."

Rocky rubbed his jaw and then licked his lips. "I'd heard they're offering five thousand dollars for Dutch. That's an awful lot of money for one man."

"It is." Dalton smiled. "So what are *we* going to do to collect that bounty?"

Rocky slapped Dalton's shoulder and then

signified that he should join him in heading back to the main drag. When they were both leaning against the corner of the stable, they surveyed the scene.

None of the other four pairs of raiders was visible, but they should all be in their positions by now at various places surrounding the bank. They wouldn't make their presence known until Dutch and Buster arrived. Jebediah was no longer outside, but as Dutch wasn't due for another half-hour, he had plenty of time to alert Nugent.

"I reckon we do nothing until Dutch rides into town," Rocky said. "Then we take on Dutch a moment after he gives the order to move in on the bank."

Dalton nodded. "I reckon we can take Dutch down while we leave the bank guards to deal with everyone else."

Rocky smiled. "That'll just leave you to point out to me the guard who shot Wesley."

"I'll be sure to do that," Dalton said, after which Rocky returned to watching the town, leaving Dalton to decide whether he would fulfill his promise.

When he'd told Rocky that Finnegan had killed Wesley, he had been trying to convince Dutch that his cover story was true and he'd had to provide a name. Now that the raid was imminent, he couldn't escape from the fact that if he identified Finnegan, Rocky would probably kill him.

He resolved that he couldn't condemn a man whose crime amounted to nothing more than being scared of the consequences of telling the truth, so he wouldn't pick him out. That resolve was tested for the first time when fifteen minutes later Finnegan came out of the bank and leaned back against the wall.

None of the guards had behaved like this before, suggesting that Nugent had formulated a plan. Rocky didn't react to this development so he presumably didn't realize that Finnegan was a guard.

Dalton hoped that the rest of Dutch's men wouldn't react either, but then Finnegan turned in their direction. Finnegan appraised them and then pushed himself away from the wall to move toward them.

A moment later Jebediah hurried out of the bank and intercepted Finnegan. The two men faced each other and with much arm waving and pointing, a vigorous debate got underway.

Dalton was too far away to work out what they were saying, but he got the impression that Jebediah was urging Finnegan to come back into the bank. Finnegan won the argument when he side-stepped around Jebediah and resumed his journey, leaving Jebediah standing with his hands on his hips. Jebediah then returned to the bank and although he adopted a casual pace, presumably to give the impression that nothing was amiss, the incident gathered Rocky's attention.

"What do you make of that?" he asked.

Dalton shrugged and then turned slowly to the advancing Finnegan, as if he'd not been paying attention to the altercation.

"I don't know," he said.

"Neither do I, but it looks like one of the bank guards is heading our way."

Dalton screwed up his eyes and then nodded. "That man is one of the guards, but as we're working to make sure Dutch fails, I don't reckon that his coming this way is anything we need to worry about."

Rocky shook his head. "We want Dutch's raid to fail, not for him to give up without trying, which he will do if his men see too much activity going on around the bank and they get spooked."

Dalton nodded and when it became clear that Finnegan was heading toward the stable, he patted Rocky's shoulder.

"You stay here and keep things calm. I'll head him off."

Without waiting for Rocky to agree he set off and to his relief, Finnegan stopped before he reached the corner of the stable.

"So Dalton's returned to be a hero," Finnegan said before Dalton reached him.

"Keep your voice down," Dalton said. "You don't know who might be listening."

"I assume you're talking about Dutch Kincaid and his outlaw gang," Finnegan said at the same volume as before. "I bet a man like you had no trouble fitting in with them."

Dalton said nothing more until he stood in front of him.

"I have fitted in because Dutch trusts me. That means a lot of eyes are on us now, and if I give a signal that something's wrong, you'll be filled with lead before you can blink twice. So stop acting like a fool."

"Nobody should think that anything's wrong. I gather that your cover story is that you were once a bank guard, so everyone will accept you talking with an old and dear friend."

"I might have been seen when I was talking with my good friend Jebediah, but now I'm talking with *you*, and I'm telling you to turn around and head back to the bank."

The implied insult made Finnegan narrow his eyes.

"I'll go when you tell me what you're doing

with your new friend." Finnegan smirked. "I've been told that's Rocky Tarrant, and he's the last person I'd expect to see walking around town with you."

Rocky appeared to be following Dalton's last instruction as he wasn't watching them and Dalton judged that he was too far away to hear what they were saying.

"He's come to town to find out what happened to his brother."

Finnegan snorted. "He doesn't need to do anything other than ask you what happened."

"We both know the truth is not as simple as telling him who pulled the trigger."

Finnegan chuckled. "You've not told him you did it!"

Finnegan had raised his voice. Fearing that Rocky might hear him Dalton stepped up closer to him, but then two riders headed toward the final building on the edge of town, showing the reason why Rocky hadn't been paying them attention. Dutch Kincaid had arrived.

"Rocky is working with me to make sure Dutch fails. That means he trusts me and if I tell him you did it, he won't wait around to hear your version of events. Now, Dutch is just about to ride into town, so move aside and we can all start working together."

Dutch and Buster had now moved out of sight on Dalton's side of the main drag so they would be facing the bank, while two of his men came out of the saloon and then sauntered along toward the bank. Dalton had no doubt that the other raiders would have seen Dutch and they would be preparing to act within moments.

Finnegan appeared to accept the urgency of the situation when he backed away a half-pace, but then with a sudden movement he lurched back. He grabbed Dalton's shoulder and spun him around. In a moment he was standing behind him with an arm wrapped around his chest.

"We won't be working together, Dalton," he said. "We're going to do this my way."

Then he dragged Dalton backward toward

the side of the main drag, an action that made the men who had come out of the saloon stop and turn to them. Two raiders who were just coming out of a mercantile and another two men who had positioned themselves opposite the bank noticed that their colleagues had stopped and they joined them in facing Dalton and Finnegan. The remaining pair was on the other side of the bank so they were unlikely to have seen this development, but they were sure to notice their colleagues' concern.

"Your way could get us all killed," Dalton said.

"It won't," Finnegan said in Dalton's ear as he drew him to a halt against the stable wall. "You don't get to be the hero today, and you sure won't get to claim the bounty on Dutch either."

Dalton shook his head. "So that's why you're acting like a damn fool, and you've already worried Dutch's men. That means you could end up stopping the raid before Dutch gives the order to start it. Everyone could get away."

"That's not going to happen."

Finnegan sounded confident making Dalton tense a moment before gunfire tore out from the roof of a building to his left. One of the raiders outside the mercantile went down clutching his chest while the other man scrambled to reach cover back in the building.

He managed only a single pace before lead hammered into his back making him stagger on for a few paces until his legs buckled and he collapsed on top of the other man. The gunfire made the men who had come out of the saloon hunker down.

They aimed at the building from where the shots had been fired, but then both men jerked around to face down the boardwalk as someone else took shots at them. Rocky was no longer visible.

Worse, the pair on Dalton's side of the main drag hurried toward a hotel on the edge of town, seemingly already abandoning all thoughts of carrying through with the bank raid. The final pair who had stationed themselves beyond the bank was no longer visible and Dutch hadn't showed himself since the shooting had started.

"I was right that you sprang the trap too quickly," Dalton said as the few townsfolk who were outside scurried for safety. "Some of Dutch's hired guns have been shot up, but Dutch is going to get away."

"Don't be so sure of that."

Jebediah came running out of the bank and then set off for the edge of town.

"I hope Jebediah's not going after Dutch on his own," Dalton said when nobody else joined him.

"He doesn't need any help to defeat this bunch of guns. Don't you go worrying about that."

Gunfire continued to blast out pinning down the men outside the saloon, but nobody was taking on the raiders who had fled. That meant Jebediah was on his own in running toward Dutch and five other gunmen.

"I'll do all the worrying I want," Dalton said, and then struggled, but he failed to shake Finnegan's arm off his chest.

"You're going nowhere. You're not getting the chance to tell Rocky any more lies about you shooting up his brother."

"I only care about helping Jebediah, just like I only cared about helping you when Wesley was about to kill you."

Finnegan snarled and then thudded a low punch into Dalton's side, the action making both men jerk forward so Dalton used the movement to drag himself forward. He failed to dislodge Finnegan, but he managed to gain a small gap between them and he kicked a heel backward.

The blow struck Finnegan beneath the knee making him grunt in pain and the pressure around Dalton's chest lessened. In a moment Dalton spun around and with the flat of his hand he delivered an uppercut to Finnegan's chin that knocked him back against the wall.

Finnegan rebounded from the wall and

with a shake of the shoulders he aimed a punch at Dalton's head, but the blow was slow in coming. Dalton easily ducked underneath Finnegan's fist and then came up to deliver a swinging punch to Finnegan's jaw that tumbled him over.

Even as Finnegan clattered to the ground, Dalton was turning on his heel and running. Jebediah had now crossed over the main drag and he was slowing down as he approached the hotel where Dalton had last seen two of the raiders.

Dalton sped up, hoping to reach him or to at least gather his attention before he made his move, but Jebediah kept going and hurried down the side of the hotel. Gunfire blasted, but thankfully it was all coming from behind him as the guards shot at the saloon where one of the raiders was now lying on his back with his chest bloodied.

The other man set off toward the saloon, and he reached the door before someone from inside the saloon gunned him down. When Dalton approached the hotel, he confirmed that the surviving raiders had all moved on.

Then, with his head down, he turned and sprinted along the side of the building. Jebediah had stopped a few paces from the back of the hotel and he was edging forward. He nodded to someone out of Dalton's line of sight before hurrying on and slipping around the corner.

Dalton moved on until he reached the spot where Jebediah had acknowledged the other guard. Jebediah's colleague was hunkered down behind a tipped-over wagon. The man was watching the scene behind the hotel, but the sight of this man made Dalton back away hurriedly before he could be seen.

Jebediah wasn't getting help from another guard. The man was Dalton's nemesis, Deputy Vaughn.

NINE

Dalton pressed his back to the wall as he gathered his thoughts. He had decided to base himself in Wilmington Point to wait for Deputy Vaughn to come for him, and it seemed as if Vaughn had duly obliged, perhaps because of the details on Dutch's Wanted poster.

Now, with Vaughn less than twenty paces away and with Dutch also not far away, Dalton couldn't help but smile. Then he drew his gun and edged forward until Vaughn came into view again.

Jebediah was walking sideways along the back of the hotel, and Vaughn was watching him giving Dalton the impression they were about to ambush Dutch and the surviving raiders. Dalton didn't want to endanger Jebediah, but he doubted that Dutch and the other five raiders would have stayed in town once it became apparent that they'd ridden into a trap.

Sure enough, Jebediah stomped to a halt and then directed a shake of the head at Vaughn. That was all Dalton needed to see and when Jebediah turned away he raised his gun. As he sighted Vaughn's chest, he recalled Walker Dodge's activities back in Harmony along with Deputy Vaughn's subsequent behavior.

He hoped this would renew his conviction that this was the right thing to do and that it was the only way out of his predicament. Then he fired. The lead scythed into the wagon a foot from Vaughn's shoulder and his second shot was no closer.

By the time he was firming his gun arm to take another shot, Vaughn had dropped down out of view. Dalton would have expected to hit a still target at such a close range. With a sigh he wondered if he was more concerned than he'd thought he would be at the prospect of shooting a man who wasn't posing him an imminent threat.

He expected that to change now that Vaughn had been shot at, but when Vaughn next came into sight he had shuffled along to the other end of the wagon where he was turned toward Jebediah. Clearly, Vaughn hadn't worked out where the shooter had fired from, and Jebediah added to his confusion by turning around and aiming his gun at someone out of Dalton's sight.

Vaughn followed Jebediah's lead and raised his gun, but before either man could fire, a rapid burst of gunfire tore out. Jebediah cried out before dropping to his knees, his gun falling from his grasp.

Vaughn shouted in defiance and then with his head down he charged out from behind the wagon. Dalton was standing in the shadows and Vaughn didn't look his way, so Dalton trained his gun on him, but with the deputy going to Jebediah's aid he didn't fire.

Vaughn reached Jebediah's side as

Jebediah toppled over to lie on his back. Vaughn didn't even slow his pace to check on him before he hurried past and, realizing that the deputy was merely chasing after the raiders and not running to help his friend, Dalton sighted Vaughn's back.

Then the corner of the hotel took Vaughn out of sight. Dalton slapped the wall in frustration and then ran after him. He scurried along the back of the hotel, and when he reached Jebediah he kneeled beside him and put a hand on his shoulder.

He started to drag him toward the nearest shade, but Jebediah didn't react. Worse, his eyes were blank and blood was already pooling beneath him. He laid Jebediah's body back down and patted his shoulder before he moved on.

When he reached the far corner of the hotel, a straggling line of six riders was galloping away. It appeared that some of them had fled straight away while others had dallied. Dutch was at the back and with the others being some distance away, he had to have been the one who had Jebediah.

Dalton loosed off a couple of shots at his fleeing form before moving along the far side of the hotel. When the main drag came into view, Vaughn was twenty paces ahead and he was hurrying toward the bank while Sheriff Coleman and several deputies moved toward him.

Everyone was calling and gesturing at each other as they reported on the progress of the gunfight. With there being so many onlookers, Dalton figured he couldn't risk taking another shot at Vaughn and he backed away to the side of the hotel.

Dutch had specified the place where they would meet up after the raid in the event of their having to split up. This hideout was beyond a ridge to the north of Wilmington Point, and as the riders were heading north, Dalton presumed he would have no difficulty in finding Dutch later.

He turned on his heel and hurried back around the hotel. He intended to head to the stable, but then he found that he didn't need to as Rocky was riding along the backs of the buildings with his horse in tow.

"It looks as if I'll have to postpone my business here for another day," Rocky said. "I suggest you do the same."

Dalton couldn't argue with that advice and in short order he mounted up. Rocky then turned his horse to the north, but Dalton raised a hand.

"Don't go that way," he said.

"Dutch is heading north."

"He is, but we don't want anyone to think we're with him. We'll find a way out of town that'll avoid anyone seeing us."

Rocky nodded and beckoned for Dalton to lead the way. Dalton murmured a promise to Jebediah's still form that he would make Dutch pay. Then he turned his horse around and hurried along the outskirts of town heading south and back along the way they'd come to Wilmington Point.

* * *

"Dutch isn't up there," Rocky said when he returned from searching the high ground.

"He's not down here either," Dalton reported with a sorry shake of the head.

Rocky slouched over the saddle and shrugged. "Then we've lost him."

"We have, but I'm not giving up that quickly."

Rocky had followed Dalton's advice and they had been cautious in their journey away from town by stopping frequently to check that they weren't being followed. They'd detected no sign of a pursuit and when they had reached a high point that overlooked the town, a distant dust cloud had been to the north.

They had presumed that Sheriff Coleman was leading a substantial number of riders in pursuit of Dutch. So they'd taken their time in moving on to the pre-arranged hide-out, but when they'd arrived a day after the failed bank raid, the area was quiet.

"I'm not giving up either. Somehow I'll

make Dutch suffer, and I still have business back in Wilmington Point." Rocky smiled. "It seems that I'm not the only one. You appeared to be having some problems with two of the bank guards."

Dalton had wondered how much Rocky had seen of his activities in Wilmington Point, but he hadn't mentioned them for fear of making Rocky think that he was concerned.

"I didn't lie when I told Dutch that I'd had some trouble when I worked for Nugent, but only the first man you saw me struggling with was a bank guard. The second man that I pursued was a deputy lawman."

Rocky rubbed his jaw. "With all those trigger-happy bank guards in Wilmington Point I could do with some help to get the man who shot up Wesley, so do you need help dealing with this deputy?"

"I might, but let's concentrate on our first problem." Dalton waited until Rocky nodded and then pointed west. "I reckon we should head back to Lerado."

"Dutch is no fool. He'll not go back there."

"He might not, but we have to start somewhere." When Rocky still looked dubious, Dalton smiled. "Besides, as we're now planning to complete unfinished business, I reckon I'd like to settle a few scores there."

Rocky chuckled, now getting his meaning and they rode on toward Dutch's base. On the way, they found no tracks or suggestions that they were heading in the right direction, and neither did they talk much.

Despite the silence, Dalton found Rocky to be better company than he had expected him to be based on the opinions about him that he'd heard in Wilmington Point. On the other hand, Finnegan had provided many of those opinions so Dalton was prepared to accept he might have misjudged him.

As Rocky appeared to have gotten involved with Dutch under duress, Dalton reckoned that if it wasn't for the fact he was keeping a terrible secret from him, they might have become friends. They took a direct route back to Lerado and at noon on the second day after leaving Dutch's hideout they caught their first sight of the town.

The state of the settlement made them draw to a halt. A fire had torn through the town and it must have happened recently as stray wafts of smoke were still rising. The blaze had destroyed most of the buildings.

It appeared to have started in the abandoned saloon that Dutch had used as his base, and then spread. The stable at the opposite edge of town appeared to be the only intact building and when with a nod to each other they moved on, the first person they came across was Kendrew McKay.

He came scurrying out of the stable and faced in their direction. Then, with an apparent show of relief, he hunched his shoulders and leaned back against the stable wall to await them.

"What happened?" Rocky called when they reached town.

"We saw some trouble," Kendrew said. "I'd assume you did, too."

"Dutch's raid failed. Half of us got shot up

before we could even get the raid underway. The ones that survived fled, but we got separated from Dutch and the others. So we headed here."

"Dutch didn't come back to Lerado, and bearing in mind what happened, it's a good job he didn't. This lawman came looking for him, and as Dutch wasn't here and we didn't know where he'd gone, he went on the rampage."

"What was his name?" Dalton asked.

"Vaughn," Kendrew said, making Rocky raise an eyebrow and Dalton wince. "I gather you know about him."

"Deputy Vaughn was waiting for us. I reckon he's tasked himself with bringing Dutch to justice."

"He didn't seem to care much about justice. When we wouldn't talk to him about what we knew he gunned down Lief and then chased down the rest of us for sport before he moved on in search of Dutch. I was the only one to survive."

"When I was last here Enoch, Lief and

Willoughby didn't exactly treat me well, but I wouldn't have wished that fate on them." Dalton narrowed his eyes. "So you're the only resident of Lerado to survive Vaughn's onslaught?"

"Sure, although I've lost my enthusiasm for the town now that there isn't a town here no more. Now that I've buried the bodies, I'm moving on."

Dalton nodded and caught Rocky's eye. "In that case I reckon we should move on with you."

"Why would you want to do that?"

"Because you're a man who passes on information to Nugent and you somehow survived what Vaughn did to this place."

Rocky grunted as he acknowledged something could be amiss in Kendrew being the town's sole survivor. He moved a pace closer to Kendrew making him sidle along the stable wall until Dalton moved to the side to block his path.

"Nugent suggested Vaughn try here." Kendrew waved an arm at both men and when neither of them moved, he barged Dalton aside and set off walking for the stable door. "Either way, if I'd known anything, I'd have told him."

"Vaughn may have gotten the idea from Nugent," Dalton shouted after him, "but he follows his own leads and his own methods, just like you do."

"I have no leads," Kendrew called as he reached the door.

"All we're asking is that you take us to Dutch."

Dalton hurried after him. He took his arm and then turned him around to face him, while Rocky moved forward to stand at Dalton's shoulder and bolster his demand.

"You're not listening to me," Kendrew said, shaking Dalton off. "I don't work for Dutch. I just keep my head down and watch what happens around me. If I see something interesting, I pass it on, provided it's worth my while."

Kendrew moved to head into the stable, but with the situation starting to irritate,

Rocky advanced quickly and grabbed Kendrew's shoulder. Then he spun him around with greater speed than Dalton had done and slammed his chest up against the stable wall.

"You're not listening to us," he muttered in Kendrew's ear. "We know all that. We're not asking you to do anything other than use the information you've gathered while keeping your head down and take us to Dutch."

Kendrew struggled, but that only encouraged Rocky to shove his arm up his back forcing Kendrew up on to his toes.

"Vaughn shot up the town and that didn't help him none," Kendrew bleated. "You can hurt me and that won't help you none either, because I don't know where Dutch will have gone."

Rocky pressed forward and mashed Kendrew's face into the wall.

"Then take your best guess as to where Dutch's gone to ground."

Kendrew gave another ineffectual struggle that failed to dislodge Rocky. Then he sighed.

"I guess I can do that," he said.

TEN

Kendrew was true to his word and he led them to a box canyon a half-day's riding from Lerado. The location seemed promising, being both secluded enough to be plausible as a hide-out, and close enough to Lerado for Dutch to have used it. They stopped a mile from the entrance, and with the scene being still Dalton turned to Kendrew.

"So this is where Dutch goes when he's not holing up in Lerado, is it?"

"As I told you, I don't know," Kendrew said with a sorry shake of the head. "I just heard one of his gang mention it."

"Then that's good enough for us." Dalton turned to Rocky. "How do you want to do this?"

"We've got no reason to suppose Dutch will have a problem with us," Rocky said. "So I reckon we just ride on into the canyon and see what happens."

Dalton nodded, and with that decision made they moved on.

"Which means you won't need me no longer," Kendrew said with a hopeful smile.

"If your guess turns out to be right, you can go," Dalton said. "If not, you're with us until you get lucky."

Kendrew grumbled to himself, but he said no more as they rode toward the entrance. They took a wide path that ensured anyone guarding the canyon would see them and when they were a hundred yards away they drew to a halt.

They waited and after a few minutes Dutch's most trusted man, Buster Lackey, raised his head over a stretch of higher ground before he dropped down out of view. A few moments later Buster reappeared with a second member of Dutch's surviving raiders, Tennessee, and this time they stayed up and nodded to them.

Rocky knew these folks better than Dalton did. He moved forward and shouted a welcome. Buster raised the flat of his hand telling him to wait before they both lowered themselves. Dalton presumed a message was being relayed back into the canyon.

Fifteen minutes passed before both men stood up and beckoned them on. Rocky took the lead and he nodded to Buster and Tennessee as they rode through the entrance. The two men were standing stooped over and they edged from foot to foot suggesting they'd suffered a bad few days since fleeing Wilmington Point.

Beyond the narrow entrance, the canyon opened up to present a broadly oval interior that was a few hundred yards across and with sides that were so steep Dalton doubted they could be scaled. Dutch had made camp against the nearly sheer western side of the canyon. He along with the three other survivors of the failed raid – Howie,

Winchester and Alphonso – stood with their backs to the rockface to await them.

"We thought you'd got shot up with the others," Dutch called when they were thirty yards away.

Rocky didn't reply until he'd dismounted and Dalton and Kendrew had gotten down from their horses to stand to either side of him.

"When the shooting started, we headed south to confuse the men who were getting ready to pursue you," he said. "As it turned out, nobody followed us, so we went to the pre-arranged place, but you weren't there."

"Then you came here." Dutch turned to Howie, who shook his head. "Despite the fact you've never been here before."

"We had help." Rocky gestured at Kendrew and he gave an apologetic shrug.

Dutch raised a foot, planted it against the side of a boulder and then leaned on his knee.

"I know for sure I never mentioned this place to the man who runs the stable in

Lerado."

Kendrew lowered his head, suggesting he didn't trust himself to speak leaving Rocky to continue explaining.

"You might not have, but that doesn't matter no more as there's no longer a town back there. Deputy Vaughn, one of the men who were doing all the shooting in Wilmington Point, went there and when he didn't find you, he shot up the town. Kendrew is the only survivor."

"I'm obliged for the information, but that doesn't answer my question. I never mentioned this place to any of you, so how come you found us here?"

Rocky spread his hands. "We didn't know you'd be here for sure, but there's no need to doubt us. We tracked you down to warn you about Vaughn."

"Maybe you did, but we've been talking and we reckon someone sold us out."

"Perhaps someone did, but don't blame us."

"Except you have a reason to turn against

us after what happened to Wesley, Dalton was the last to join us and he was seen talking with the bank guards, and Kendrew knows more about us than he's let on." Dutch lowered his foot from the boulder and then stalked around it to stand before them. "So which one of you did it?"

Dutch's three gunmen edged their hands toward their holsters as they awaited Rocky's answer. Dalton reckoned that if he went for his gun, he'd be shot before he finished the move, but thankfully he didn't need to respond to the threat when Kendrew broke ranks first.

With a screeched cry of anguish he turned on his heel and scurried for his horse. All three gunmen along with Dutch drew their guns. The three gunmen leveled their weapons on Rocky and Dalton leaving Dutch to deal with Kendrew.

He shouted a warning that Kendrew didn't heed and then blasted a shot into the ground between Kendrew and his horse. Kendrew skidded to a halt and then turned to the canyon at the entrance, but as two men were on look-out there, he appeared to accept with a sigh that there was no way out.

He stopped searching for an escape route and turned to Dutch, who indicated that Howie should bring him over. Howie nodded and walked in a long circle until he was standing behind Kendrew. With a nudge of his gun in the back he encouraged Kendrew to walk on until he stood in front of Dutch.

"I didn't sell you out," Kendrew said with his head lowered. "The only reason I'm alive is I got lucky when Deputy Vaughn came looking for you."

"Where is this lawman now?"

"I don't know, and I don't ever want to meet him again."

Dutch nodded and then tapped the heel of his boot against the boulder, as if he was thinking about the answer.

"You'll have to if you've led him here."

"I didn't."

"You got lucky when you survived, but

maybe that was just our bad luck and the lawman let you live so that you'd lead him to us."

"I had no intention of coming here until those two forced me to take a guess as to where you'd gone."

Kendrew directed an imploring look at Rocky that asked him to back up his story. Then he moved on to sneer at Dalton that appeared to acknowledge that he could save himself by casting doubt on him.

"That much of his story is true, but we've been careful," Dalton said, stepping forward. "We've spent the last few days looking over our shoulders and I'm sure that we haven't been followed. I can't be so sure that you haven't."

Dutch muttered something under his breath and then walked past Kendrew to advance on Dalton.

"Don't make accusations about my actions. The only people under suspicion here are you three, and I reckon you can answer my questions first."

Dutch signified for Winchester to bring Dalton to him while Alphonso took it upon himself to advance on Rocky, who gave a slight nod, so Dalton moved on before his escort could reach him and with a pleasant smile on his face he spread his hands.

"I'll be glad to answer your questions, but if you're looking for someone to blame, you got it right the first time." Dalton smiled. "Kendrew works for Nugent. Everything Kendrew finds out goes straight to him, for a price."

Kendrew turned to Dalton, his mouth opening wide in shock and reinforcing Dalton's claim. Then he pointed at him, his finger shaking as he clearly prepared to voice a counter-accusation. The three gunmen picked up on Kendrew's likely guilt and turned their guns on him while Dutch shook his head sadly.

"Shoot him," he said simply.

Kendrew clamped his lips closed with whatever he might have uttered left unsaid. Then he barged Howie aside and broke into a run toward his horse. Howie stumbled a pace to the side before going down on one knee while Winchester and Alphonso followed Kendrew with their guns as he set off on a possibly hopeless quest to reach his horse.

Dalton had only hoped to sow confusion and he hadn't expected Dutch to take such decisive action immediately against Kendrew. Wasting no time, he threw his hand to his holster.

He drew and aimed at Winchester, and to his delight Rocky drew his gun and aimed at Alphonso. Two gunshots rang out, the sounds echoing against the rockface. Dalton's shot caught Winchester in the side making him stand up straight until a second shot to the neck downed him, while Rocky dispatched Alphonso with a single shot to the side of the head.

Dalton then jerked his gun around to aim at Dutch, but the leader was already diving for cover behind the boulder. Dalton took aim at his diving form, but then stilled his fire when Howie righted himself and swung his gun arm around toward him.

Howie loosed off a wild shot before Rocky got him in his sights and hammered lead into his chest, while a second shot to the chest from Dalton a moment later made their opponent tip over sideways. Then Rocky and Dalton turned back to the boulder where Dutch had gone to ground.

They trained their guns on either side of the rock waiting for him to show, but Dutch stayed down. The rapid change in fortunes didn't appear to mollify Kendrew as he had already given up on his attempt to reach his horse and he scurried off across the canyon.

Dalton was surprised that he didn't head to the entrance, and he got an explanation for his behavior soon enough when the distant forms of Buster and Tennessee came riding toward them. Clearly, the gunfire had attracted their attention and now they were galloping into the canyon.

Dalton got Rocky's attention and pointed them out. As the two men would be here within minutes, with gestures and mouthed comments they agreed that they needed to subdue Dutch before the riders arrived and their opponents had the chance to turn the tables on them.

They split up with Dalton heading to one side of the boulder and Rocky moving to the other. They both edged forward with their guns thrust out, but their adversary must have pressed himself tightly to the rock as Dalton reached a point nearly side-on to the boulder without seeing him.

Then, to his horror, he discovered that Dutch could have fooled them. A narrow and dry rill ran from the boulder to the rockface and it was deep enough for a man to take cover in it and even crawl along it.

There was nowhere close to the gash in the ground that Dutch could have reached without being seen, but the rill increased the number of places where he could be hiding. Dalton gestured at Rocky and then pointed at the rill, and with a scowl Rocky accepted that Dalton could be right.

Then Rocky hurried forward to the boulder. He shook his head and then trained his gun on the rill. As the gash ran along the ground past Dalton giving him only a limited view of the interior and Rocky could see down some of its length, Rocky took the lead in edging forward.

Dalton swung his gun from side to side as he waited for any tell-tale changes in the light level that might offer a clue as to where Dutch was hiding along the twenty-yard length of the rill. When Rocky covered five slow paces without him reacting, Dalton winced with concern.

Buster and Tennessee were galloping ever closer and they'd now covered over half the distance from the entrance. He judged that they would be within firing range in around another minute so abandoning his cautious method, Dalton put his head down and broke into a run.

He presumed Dutch must have made his way along to the end nearest the rockface, and in five long paces he reached a point where most of the length was visible. As Dutch wasn't there, he threw himself to the ground, rolled and then tipped over into the rill.

He slithered down the side and slapped down on the bottom on his chest. Then he turned toward the boulder. As he'd hoped, Dutch was ahead of him and pressed tightly against the side, but he'd heard Dalton's scrambling approach and he was already training his gun on him.

Dutch fired, but his shot sliced into the side of the rill, Dalton's rapid movement having clearly surprised him. While Dutch steadied his aim, Dalton swung his gun arm forward. His rapid shot caught Dutch's arm making him flinch.

Even better, it made Dutch waste his second shot into the bottom of the rill. Then Dutch swung around to find Rocky carrying out the same action as Dalton had done of running and then leaping into the rill.

Even before he'd hit the bottom, Rocky fired, catching Dutch in the stomach and giving Dalton enough time to take careful aim and hammer a shot into Dutch's side. Dutch cried out and then slammed chest first against the side of the rill before sliding down to the bottom.

Both men trained their guns on his form. When Dutch didn't move again, Dalton scrambled forward and turned him over. He noted Dutch's dead eyes.

"It seems that we've got our man," he said.

"Unfortunately for Dutch, he didn't pick a good place to hide," Rocky said with approval.

Dalton started to nod, but then rapid approaching footfalls sounded, presumably from Buster and Tennessee.

"Except we're in Dutch's position now," Dalton said with a wince. "So it could turn out to be unfortunate for us, too."

ELEVEN

Dalton raised his head, and then ducked back down when Buster snapped up his gun arm to aim at him. Buster and Tennessee had dismounted and they were now in the same positions that Rocky and Dalton had been in a few moments earlier on either side of the boulder.

Dalton gestured to Rocky to watch for either of them approaching from the left while Dalton concentrated on the right. They shuffled backward to hunker down with their backs to each other while they awaited the gunmen's next move.

Around fifteen minutes passed in silence. It was late in the day, but, as it wouldn't get dark for a while, the gunmen could afford to wait them out. When Rocky started to shuffle uncomfortably Dalton accepted they had to make a move before boredom and cramps made them lose concentration and they suffered the same fate as Dutch had.

He nudged Rocky and with a resigned nod Rocky agreed they had to make the first move. Using gestures alone they agreed to split up and move as far away from each other as they could while staying hidden in the rill.

Rocky signified that if Dalton covered him he reckoned he could leave the gash in the ground at speed and then run quickly enough to reach the boulder. With that plan in place, they dropped down on to their chests and crawled along the bottom of the rill until they reached a point where its gentle curve was starting to take them out of each other's sight.

Then they got up on to their haunches and Rocky provided a count down from three. The moment Rocky lowered his last finger he jumped to his feet and moved to vault out of the rill while Dalton raised his head and slapped his gun hand on the edge of the rill.

He aimed at the last place he'd seen the nearest gunman, but he stilled his fire as neither of the men was visible. As Rocky clambered out on to flat land, Dalton raised his head higher and found that the gunmen had been trying a move of their own.

Buster was snaking his way along the ground toward the place where they had been hiding until a few minutes ago, while Tennessee had slipped behind the boulder so that he could cover his colleague. Only Tennessee's arm was visible as he aimed at Rocky.

Dalton blasted off a shot at him that sliced into rock making Tennessee flinch before he jerked his gun around toward Dalton. A quick shot hit the dirt several feet to Dalton's side, but with little to aim at, Dalton took his time in firing.

Before he could shoot again, a second shot hammered into the edge of the rill landing so close it kicked dirt into Dalton's eyes. Dalton fired blind and then shook his head.

When his vision cleared, he was facing Tennessee's aimed gun.

Rocky was pounding along toward the boulder so he thrust his head down below the edge. His quick action saved him from Tennessee's gunshot that sliced into the dirt where his head had been a moment ago.

Then he dropped down on to hands and knees and fast-crawled along the bottom of the rill so that he could come up in a position where he would have a clearer view of his target. When he'd covered five yards, he got back up on his haunches.

He figured he would also be closer to Buster, who had been crawling toward him, but as Rocky would be moments away from reaching the boulder, he jerked his head up straight away. Even as he swung his gun toward the boulder he registered that Buster had moved quickly and he was now only a yard away from the edge.

Buster was heading to a position that was four feet to Dalton's left, but Dalton's appearance made him speed his approach.

Buster got up on his knees and then scrambled toward Dalton forcing Dalton to ignore Tennessee and turn his gun on the nearer man.

Before he could fire, Buster launched himself forward and his outstretched hands caught Dalton around the shoulders knocking him backward. As gunfire tore out over by the boulder, both men went tumbling down into the bottom of the rill where Dalton landed on his back with Buster lying sprawled on top of him.

Then their momentum made them both roll up the other side letting Dalton get the upper hand. Dalton was still clutching his gun and he thrust the barrel in toward Buster's chest, but his opponent registered what he was trying to do and he squirmed while kicking up, knocking Dalton aside.

Buster followed him and flattened him to the bottom of the rill, his weight blasting all the air out of Dalton's lungs. Then, while more gunfire tore out as Rocky and Tennessee traded shots, Buster grabbed

Dalton's arms and sought to raise them so he could pin him down.

Dalton was still struggling to get his breath and he couldn't stop his arms from being moved, but then a gunshot blasted. Buster stiffened and that let Dalton realize that the pressure on his arms had resulted in a shot being loosed off at close quarters.

He flexed his gun arm and then twisted his hand to jab the gun into Buster's stomach before firing a second time. Buster tensed and then flopped down to lie over him, his heavy form thudding down on Dalton's chest and trapping his gun arm.

Dalton tried to buck him, but he failed to shift Buster's body so he sought to squirm out from under him. Then the light level on the side of the rill changed, and a man's form loomed up into view. Dalton dragged his arm out from under Buster's dead weight and raised his gun, but then he registered that Rocky was above him.

"You can carry on resting up down there," Rocky said with a smile. "It seems that we've dealt with them all now."

Dalton returned a smile, but he didn't relax until he'd clambered out of the rill and confirmed that they had wiped out the surviving members of the Dutch Kincaid gang. He finished his perusal facing Dutch's body.

"He doesn't look like the fearsome bandit we'd all heard about anymore," he said.

"Maybe not, but he does look like five thousand dollars."

Dalton nodded, but then uttered a long sigh. "All we have to do to get our hands on that bounty is take him back to Wilmington Point."

"Your tone sounds as if you reckon that might be tough."

"It could be. If you were to just ride into town to claim the bounty and someone recognizes you from Dutch's failed raid, you'd be sure to face problems."

Rocky narrowed his eyes. "Then I'll just have to rely on you to vouch that I was working with you to bring down Dutch."

Dalton raised a hand in a placating gesture. "Don't worry about that. I'll speak up for you, but I can only do that if I get the chance. Deputy Vaughn is out there looking for Dutch, but I'm sure he'll settle for just getting me."

Rocky jutted his jaw as he thought about the problems they might still face and then pointed across the canyon, drawing Dalton's attention to Kendrew's distant form. Kendrew had fled when the gunfight had erupted, but he had stopped at a safe point a few hundred yards away. He was now loitering at the side of the canyon seemingly torn between returning and heading for the entrance.

"I reckon we might still have a use for Kendrew," Rocky said. "If we face problems, he can take the body into Wilmington Point for us."

Dalton nodded and they set off across the canyon toward him. At first, Kendrew backed away, but he must have registered that only Rocky and Dalton were approaching as he stopped and then moved on to join them.

"I'm mighty pleased to see you two prevailed," he called when they were a few dozen yards apart.

"We did, and with no help from you," Rocky said.

Kendrew shrugged. "I never wanted to join you on this expedition and I never said I'd help you."

"In which case you did exactly what you claimed you'd do, and now we're in possession of a dead outlaw who has a substantial bounty on his head."

Rocky said no more until he and Dalton were standing before Kendrew, his silence letting Kendrew work the situation out for himself.

"You wouldn't have found Dutch without my help," Kendrew said cautiously.

"We wouldn't, and we intend to show our gratitude. So I'm sure you'll want to stay with us until we can hand in Dutch's body."

"I sure will." Kendrew rubbed his hands as

if he were now searching for ways he could make himself useful. "I'll round up the horses and deal with them. Then I'll see what provisions Dutch's men had on them and get some food cooking."

Rocky stood aside and with mock courtesy gestured for Kendrew to get to work. When Kendrew moved on across the canyon, Dalton and Rocky both smiled and then followed on after him.

For the next hour, as the light level dropped, they busied themselves with making camp. They agreed to keep a cautious eye on the entrance, but with the canyon being in a secluded place they didn't take any special precautions.

Even so, with all the bodies lying close to their camp and with an uncertain few days ahead, everyone was pensive. They ate in silence. Afterward, they didn't talk for long and sleep took some time to come for them all.

In the morning, as they prepared to move out, they all still acted pensively. They agreed to take only Dutch's body, figuring that Sheriff Coleman could collect the rest of the bodies after they'd claimed the bounty.

So they draped Dutch over a spare horse. Then, with Kendrew leading the horse, they rode off.

"Which route should we take to town?" Rocky asked when they closed on the entrance.

"I reckon we should head directly there," Dalton said. "Vaughn will probably expect Dutch to put as much distance as he can between himself and Wilmington Point, so I reckon the closer we get to town, the safer we'll be."

"Provided he's still looking for Dutch and not for you."

Dalton sighed, acknowledging this was his greatest fear. He assumed Vaughn had become interested in finding Dutch because Dalton's crime had appeared on Dutch's Wanted poster and he hoped that finding the outlaw could lead him to his quarry.

"If he appears, I'll deal with him."

"If that's what you want, I'll let you take the lead, but remember I still need your help to identify this Finnegan O'Doyle."

Dalton sighed again, as Rocky brought up his other major concern. With all his other worries he'd managed to avoid thinking about how he would deal with a matter that he couldn't postpone for much longer.

Finnegan had acted in a foolish manner on several occasions, but Dalton didn't reckon his actions were sufficiently bad that he could justify fingering him as Wesley's killer. More important, while they had been together Rocky had behaved in a decent manner and they had helped each other several times, so he figured he owed him the truth.

How Rocky would react when he learned that truth Dalton didn't know so he resolved to spend the journey to Wilmington Point getting to know him better so that he could lessen the impact of the revelation.

"I'll be sure to help you understand the full story," Dalton said, making Rocky nod.

Then, as they were approaching the entrance to the canyon, Rocky rode on ahead to take the lead. When he was a few horse-lengths ahead, Kendrew rode on to join Dalton and then shrugged.

"Before Deputy Vaughn shot up Lerado, I heard some stories about what happened in Wilmington Point," he said. "I didn't hear anyone say that Finnegan O'Doyle killed Rocky's brother."

"Who did you hear killed him?"

"I didn't hear that, but I did hear that you had some problems back there before you tried to infiltrate Dutch's gang."

"You hear plenty, but hearing is different to actually being there."

Kendrew looked as if he was prepared to say more, but Dalton couldn't help but think that Kendrew's comment had been honest. Kendrew didn't know who had killed Wesley, but he was starting to suspect that something was odd about Dalton's version of events.

Dalton didn't welcome the thought of

dealing with that problem now and he moved ahead of Kendrew. In single file, they headed through the entrance, although Rocky slowed when they approached the stretch of higher ground where Buster and Tennessee had first seen them.

Then Rocky signified that Dalton and Kendrew should wait before he moved on slowly over the rise. He had yet to reach the summit when he jerked his head down and turned his horse quickly. A gunshot tore out followed by rapid shots that hurried him on his way back to them.

"I didn't see anyone, but I reckon the firing came from over there," Rocky said when he joined them.

Rocky pointed along the side of the canyon. Dalton recalled that the ground there provided plenty of cover and he frowned, but before he could respond, a clear voice rang out from beyond the entrance.

"This is Deputy Vaughn," the voice called. "You folks will come out with your hands up or you'll die in there."

TWELVE

Dalton signified that Kendrew should stay back while he and Rocky dismounted. Then they hurried over to the higher ground where they lay down on their bellies in the same positions that Buster and Tennessee had adopted.

This position gave them a good view of most of the surrounding land, and that confirmed Rocky's observation that the land to the right was a blind spot where Vaughn had probably gone to ground.

"As we agreed earlier, I'll deal with him," Dalton said. He eyed the terrain beyond the entrance as he tried to work out how he could get closer to Vaughn. "I may need some covering fire."

"You'll get it, but we might still be able to walk away from this without further gunfire," Rocky said. "Vaughn didn't say anything about you, so he might not know you're here."

"You could be right and he may only think he's about to launch an ambush on Dutch, but in my experience there's no reasoning with Vaughn." Dalton shrugged. "I guess trying won't do no harm."

Rocky nodded and then edged forward. He raised himself slightly.

"Dutch Kincaid is dead, as are the rest of his raiders," he shouted.

They both waited and long moments passed before Vaughn spoke up, his voice now clearly coming from a point around fifty yards away to their right and at ground level.

"What's that matter?"

"It means you have no reason to shoot at law-abiding men. We're bounty hunters and we dealt with Dutch. Now we're heading to Wilmington Point with his body to get our reward. We'd be obliged if you'd let us do that."

"You're not listening to me, so this is your last warning. Come out with your hands up or die in there."

Rocky slapped the ground in frustration and then shuffled back to join Dalton.

"It seems you're right. There's no reasoning with Vaughn."

"At least you got to see that for yourself. Now leave me to get us out of here."

Dalton waited until Rocky nodded and then turned his thoughts to how he could sneak up on Vaughn. Fallen shale covered the first fifty feet of the climb up the side of the canyon ensuring that the incline at the bottom of the slope was slight.

So he figured he could easily reach a position where he would be above Vaughn. Back in Wilmington Point, he had been ineffective when he'd gotten Vaughn in his sight, but with a roll of his shoulders he vowed to himself that this time he wouldn't fail.

Then he dropped down on to his chest and snaked along behind the higher ground. After a dozen yards he reached the bottom of the incline where he raised himself. Then on hands and knees he climbed up the loose rock.

He followed a diagonal route that took him closer to the entrance while gaining height. He kept one eye on the area where he reckoned Vaughn had been when he had shouted his demands.

As he was familiar with Vaughn's sneaky behavior, he also sought out other places where the deputy could have moved to. Slowly he maneuvered himself along, and the terrain beyond the entrance came into view.

When most of the land to the right was visible he stopped. Rocky was lying just below the summit of the higher ground and didn't appear as if he was paying attention to Dalton. Farther back in the canyon, Kendrew was hunched forward in the saddle and shaking his head in apparent disapproval of their plan.

Dalton nodded to Rocky and indicated with spread hands that he'd yet to see Vaughn. Then he moved on. He figured that after another twenty yards Rocky wouldn't be visible anymore.

As they had heard Vaughn clearly when he'd shouted his demands, he also reckoned he was close to the place where the deputy had been. He stopped, found a length of flat rock to lie on and searched for potential hiding-places.

Several boulders were below along with a stretch of undulating land, but a massive boulder drew his attention. The angular rock appeared to have tumbled down the side of the canyon and it was large enough to cover Vaughn even if he stood up and moved around.

It also provided a clear view of the ground beyond the rise where Rocky was waiting. When several minutes passed with the scene remaining still, he turned back to Rocky. He pointed at him and then put his hands around his mouth and mimed shouting. When Rocky nodded, he shuffled back around to await the result.

"We've been talking," Rocky shouted. "We don't believe you're a lawman, so we're not following your orders. Either you leave and let us take Dutch's body to Wilmington Point, or you'll have to come in and deliver on that warning."

"You're not going anywhere," Vaughn shouted. "There's no way out of this canyon, except for this one."

Rocky waited for further instructions and Dalton raised a calming hand. He couldn't be sure, but he was now even more convinced that Vaughn was hiding behind the large boulder. He worked out the safest path to the boulder, but he figured that at some stage on the trip he would probably dislodge one of the many loose rocks and alert Vaughn.

On the other hand, Vaughn was devious and having stated that he was prepared to wait them out, he was likely to do the opposite. Sure enough, a minute later a shadow flickered beyond the near side of the boulder suggesting Vaughn was preparing to make a move.

Dalton leveled his gun on the spot where he expected Vaughn to appear and with his elbows planted on the rock, he took calming breaths. The shadow appeared again. This time it didn't move away, although it edged from side to side, giving the impression that Vaughn was just out of sight and he was examining the lie of the land as he planned his next action.

Dalton's hopes were growing that Vaughn would soon come into full view when Rocky spoke up back in the entrance. Then Kendrew shouted something. He couldn't hear what they were saying, but the shadow darted back out of sight and in irritation Dalton noted that Kendrew had ridden forward to join Rocky, who was up on his haunches remonstrating with him.

Kendrew ignored whatever Rocky told him and with Dutch's body in tow, he moved his horse on over the rise and through the entrance. Rocky moved to follow him, but then thought better of putting himself in Vaughn's line of sight and he limited himself to muttering ever more urgent demands for him to come back, but Kendrew rode on.

Dalton raised a hand to Rocky telling him not to risk following Kendrew. Whatever Kendrew's motivation was for leaving, he figured it was likely to bring Vaughn out into the open. Accordingly, Kendrew faced the boulder, after which he raised a hand from the reins and rode on in that direction.

"I know what you really want, Vaughn, and you've got it wrong," he shouted.

"Don't come no closer," Vaughn shouted from behind the boulder.

Kendrew ignored him and rode on at a steady pace.

"When you rode into Lerado you claimed you were looking for Dutch Kincaid, but you said plenty of things back then and I've been thinking. I now reckon you were looking for another man who you reckon was riding with Dutch."

"You don't know nothing."

"Except I know everyone who was with Dutch is now dead, including the man you want, Dalton."

Kendrew drew his horse to a halt at a spot that was directly below Dalton. He sat tall in the saddle, appearing confident, presumably due to Vaughn's reaction after his revelation.

"Dalton *is* Dutch!" Vaughn shouted.

"Like I said, you got it wrong." Kendrew gestured back at the horse behind him. "This man is Dutch and the picture on his Wanted poster proves his identity. Dalton is lying dead back in the canyon."

Vaughn didn't reply immediately, the delay giving Dalton the impression he was seriously considering Kendrew's claim.

"Get down off your horse and keep your hands away from your holster," Vaughn said after a while. "Then lead the horse on and show me."

Kendrew did as Vaughn ordered, making

Dalton scowl as that wouldn't bring Vaughn out of hiding, but Kendrew must have been aware of the situation as he stopped five paces away from the boulder leaving the body in clear view. Then he backed away to stand beside Dutch and raised his head.

"Have you seen enough?" he called.

"I can't make out the face," Vaughn said.

Dalton expected Vaughn would then demand that Kendrew bring Dutch closer, but to his surprise Vaughn walked out from the boulder and headed straight toward the horse. Dalton followed him with his gun, but he held his fire as Vaughn would be even closer to him when he reached Kendrew.

With firm strides Vaughn strode up to the horse, barged Kendrew aside and yanked Dutch's head up, his brisk actions confirming that he had believed that Dalton and Dutch were the same man. Unfortunately, when Kendrew came to a halt, he stood directly between Dalton and his target.

Then, with Vaughn having turned his back on Kendrew for the first time, Kendrew edged his hand toward his holster. Even as Dalton was smiling at Kendrew's cunning, Vaughn flinched and then turned around, somehow detecting Kendrew's attempted deception before he could carry through with his plan.

Vaughn snapped up his gun arm and fired, shooting Kendrew low in the chest before Kendrew had even touched leather. Kendrew stumbled forward, receiving a second shot to the chest that dropped him.

Then Vaughn turned to the entrance and blasted off a shot even though Rocky had stayed back and he wouldn't be visible to him. The gunfire spooked both the horses and they bustled forward, but with Kendrew no longer blocking his view, Dalton fired.

His shot kicked dirt beyond Vaughn's form and it made him go to one knee, but then the horse carrying Dutch's body skittered toward him making him leap aside. Dalton fired again, but that shot landed even farther away from his target as Vaughn rolled away to the bottom of the slope where the low-lying land took him out of view.

Dalton still reckoned Vaughn was trapped down there and he had shown no sign of being aware of where the shooting was coming from. Rocky added to his problems when he hurried out from the entrance while firing on the run.

Vaughn blasted a shot at him. Then he came out from his cover sprinting with his head down. Only Vaughn's hat and the top of his back was visible, but Dalton still fired. The shot sliced into rock and then Vaughn gained the safety of the boulder.

Vaughn fired from behind his cover making Rocky hurry back out of sight where he hunkered down at the bottom of the slope. Then, with the horses moving out of sight, the scene returned to stillness.

Despite the setback, Dalton still reckoned he and Rocky had the advantage, and now that Rocky had moved forward, Dalton no longer felt he should take Vaughn on alone. Rocky raised himself to get Dalton's attention and then pointed at the far side of the boulder.

Dalton got his meaning that they should try to trap Vaughn with a pincer movement. He stood up and moved on, this time not trying to stay silent as he aimed to reach his destination quickly.

He had halved the distance when Rocky waved at him. Then Rocky fired twice before hurrying forward and firing again. No returning gunfire came from Vaughn, and a few moments later the deputy appeared from behind the boulder.

He had mounted up and was galloping away from the canyon. Trailing behind him was the horse carrying Dutch's body.

THIRTEEN

"I thought the only thing Vaughn cared about was getting you," Rocky said when Dalton joined him at ground level.

Dalton hunkered down beside Kendrew's body and confirmed he was dead.

"Vaughn has pursued me for months and he's never relented for even a moment," Dalton said. "But I guess he found the thought of claiming the bounty on Dutch's head more exciting than capturing me."

"You were right that Vaughn sure is a devious varmint, so perhaps he's only bluffing and he'll double back to see if your body really is in the canyon."

With the dust cloud that Vaughn had left behind dispersing and the deputy no longer being visible, Dalton sighed.

"I'm guessing that he'd convinced himself that I was Dutch rather than that I was riding with his outlaw gang, and when he saw Dutch's face he accepted he'd got it wrong. Either way, he can come back later and check out the canyon."

Rocky kicked at the ground. "That'll be after he's gotten his hands on our bounty."

Dalton nodded, but then slapped Rocky's shoulder.

"The rule Vaughn is planning to use here is that the man who rides into Wilmington Point with Dutch's body gets to claim the bounty on him, so I reckon we just need to make sure that man isn't Vaughn."

Rocky frowned. "Even with you confirming my story that I've been helping you undermine Dutch, if it comes down to making a ruling, I don't trust Sheriff Coleman to decide in my favor."

"We'll worry about that problem after we've solved the first problem of getting the body back."

Rocky bent down to pat Kendrew's back and then gave a determined nod.

"I guess plenty of bad things can happen to a sneaky lawman between here and Wilmington Point."

Dalton chuckled and with that agreement, Dalton took Kendrew's arms and Rocky took his legs. They moved him closer to the rocks, after which they murmured a quick promise to return later and ensure he received a proper burial.

Then they hurried back into the canyon to collect their horses. Within a few minutes they were riding away along the route Vaughn had taken. Vaughn had set off using the same route that they'd used to reach the box canyon suggesting he'd followed their tracks from Lerado, but they failed to catch sight of Vaughn riding ahead, and when after a half-hour they lost his trail they headed toward the abandoned town.

In mid-afternoon, they approached their first destination, but Vaughn wasn't in Lerado and they found no sign that he had stopped there either. This town was on the most direct route between the canyon and Wilmington Point, so while they rested their horses they debated their options.

As Vaughn had given them the slip quickly, they presumed that even before he'd launched his assault he'd already had a plan in mind to confound any pursuers. That meant if they scouted around in search of him and his tracks, they would probably fail.

On the other hand, if Vaughn was being stealthy in his movements that would slow him down and they were probably already closer to their ultimate destination than he was. No matter what route to Wilmington Point he took, eventually he would have to try to enter the town.

So they only had to ensure they reached the town quickly and then get into a position to waylay him. The issue of how they would intercept him when only the two of them would have to patrol all the approaches to town was another problem they decided to postpone until later.

They set off from Lerado and in an open manner rode on toward Wilmington Point. On the way, they agreed on the story they would relate if they were to meet Sheriff Coleman and the posse who had chased after Dutch and who could still be searching for him.

Dalton would reveal that Nugent had recruited him to infiltrate Dutch's gang and that he'd sought help from Rocky who wanted to bring down Dutch to avenge his brother's needless death. They would explain their success in finding and then killing Dutch and the remnants of his gang.

Then they would relate their failure to keep hold of his body, although they would provide only sketchy details about the incident in which Vaughn had attacked them in case that gave Dalton any problems. Dalton was grateful that Rocky accepted this final element of the story, but the possibility that they might soon meet the sheriff brought into focus the fact that before long he would no longer have a choice about when and how he should reveal the truth about Wesley's demise.

He resolved that when they made camp for the night he'd stop putting off the problem and discuss the matter with Rocky. So when they settled down after a long day's traveling, he rehearsed in his mind several ways to explain what had happened.

Unfortunately, none of the ways sounded anything less than damning for him and after brooding for a while he drifted off to sleep without finding a solution to his dilemma. The next day followed the same routine in which they rode quickly, but again they saw no sign of Vaughn.

They reached Wilmington Creek late in the day and settled down at a high point where the length of the water toward the distant Wilmington Point was visible. Dalton had passed this spot when he'd first ridden toward town and he knew they should be able to reach Wilmington Point before noon tomorrow.

As he reckoned he couldn't put off his unwelcome task any longer, while they were eating he broached the subject of what Rocky would do when he met Finnegan. By way of an answer Rocky merely drew his gun and snarled, so Rocky's obvious anger stopped Dalton from even thinking about how he could reveal the truth.

He didn't try to broach the subject again that night and when they rode on the next morning, Dalton couldn't help but feel guilty. His guilty feeling became even more acute when in mid-morning they rode over a rise and Finnegan was loitering beside the water ahead.

As both men drew back behind the rise before Finnegan noticed them, Dalton had to gulp to fight down a nauseous feeling. Then they debated their next actions.

"That man's one of Nugent's bank guards," Dalton said, "and he's waiting in the same place as when I first came across him. That could mean he's again waiting here in the hope of waylaying someone."

Rocky nodded. "Nugent won't know that Dutch is dead, so he could be fearing that he'll return to carry out another raid."

"You could be right, but on the other hand, the guard is another sneaky varmint so he doesn't have to be following Nugent's orders. I reckon we should avoid him."

Rocky frowned and Dalton couldn't blame him, as his suggestion hadn't sounded convincing to his own ears. As it was now likely that Rocky would ask for the guard's name, Dalton resolved to provide it and then use the opportunity that revelation afforded to move on and explain the rest, but Rocky shrugged.

"Even if we hadn't come across this man, we'd soon have to pick a spot to lie in wait for Vaughn, so I reckon this is a good time to start waiting." Rocky pointed farther along the rise at a grouping of three boulders. "We should hole up over there and watch what he does."

Dalton nodded and they rode along below the summit of the rise on the opposite side to Finnegan. When they reached the boulders, they had an excellent view of the terrain both along the side of the creek and farther inland.

So they dismounted and moved on to lie on their chests between two of the boulders. Finnegan had now moved position so that he stood directly below them. He was facing upriver in an alert manner that suggested he could have heard or perhaps even caught sight of them.

Beyond Finnegan, the slope down to Wilmington Creek was as steep as Dalton remembered it, and with the ground still being muddy it looked as treacherous as it had done when Jebediah had nearly drowned. The path up to the boulders was equally steep and from their elevated position, Dalton could see how Jebediah had managed to use the cover afforded by the terrain to sneak up on him unseen.

Rocky leaned forward to appraise the land below them and nodded in approval of this being a good place to mount an ambush, if

Vaughn happened to come this way. Then they settled down to await developments, and they didn't have to wait for long.

After standing for a while Finnegan slapped a thigh, as if he'd made a decision and then set off walking up the slope toward them. He kept his head down as he picked out an upward path, suggesting he was seeking out high ground to survey the scene rather than that he knew they were hiding there. So both men edged back from the boulders and stood with their backs to the rock.

"There's nowhere for us to hide up here," Dalton said. "He's sure to see us."

"I don't reckon that's a problem," Rocky said. "If people from Wilmington Point start hearing our story about how we're the men who killed Dutch, it'll improve our chances of stopping Vaughn claiming the bounty."

Dalton shook his head. "I don't reckon he'll side with me."

Rocky sighed as he pondered and then nodded.

"Now that you mention it, I recognize that man now. He's the guard you were arguing with just before Dutch rode into town." Rocky smiled. "Who is he?"

Dalton winced, now regretting the many times he'd avoided opening up about his terrible secret, especially now that he couldn't avoid talking about it and the situation ensured that he wouldn't have the time to explain himself properly.

"That's not as important as just avoiding him," he said, his voice croaking. "We should just move on toward town and pick a different spot to waylay Vaughn."

Rocky furrowed his brow. "What's wrong?"

Dalton opened his mouth, but no words would come and worse, Finnegan's footfalls had stopped, suggesting he'd heard them talking. Dalton raised a warning hand and then slipped his head between the boulders.

Sure enough, Finnegan wasn't visible below. He swung back while shaking his head only to find that Finnegan was stepping out from behind the far side of the boulder.

"I thought I saw someone coming downriver, but I never expected it'd be you," Finnegan said. Then he turned to Rocky. "As Rocky is still with you, he must have believed the lies you've no doubt been telling him."

"I've told Rocky no lies," Dalton said, as a feeling of foreboding hit him.

Finnegan chuckled. "Which means you haven't told him the truth either."

Rocky stepped back to keep them both in view. "What's he talking about, Dalton?"

Dalton took a deep breath and then faced Rocky. "This is difficult for me and I wouldn't have chosen this moment to mention it for the first time. He's talking about the unfortunate death of your brother and how it came to happen."

"You mean this man knows who killed. . . ?" Rocky flinched, as if he'd picked up on the reason for Dalton's concern. Then, without waiting for Dalton's answer, he turned to

Finnegan. "Who are you?"

Finnegan took a long step forward. "I'm Finnegan O'Doyle. I was the only witness when Dalton gunned down your brother in cold blood."

Rocky opened and closed his mouth without making a sound and then turned back to Dalton, who provided a placating smile as he sought the right words to explain himself. Dalton must have looked guilty as Rocky roared with anger and then threw himself at him.

With his arms outstretched Rocky caught Dalton around the chest and carried him backward into the boulder. Dalton's back slammed into the rock, but he made no effort to defend himself as Rocky pressed him flat.

"Look me in the eye and tell me that's not true," he said.

"It isn't like it sounds," Dalton said.

Dalton winced when he accepted that explanation was a weak one, but before he could say anything more Rocky grabbed his right shoulder and hurled him into the gap between the two boulders. Dalton came to a halt standing on the edge of the slope.

"I don't ever want to see your face again, so stay facing that way," Rocky said. "Then I'm shooting you in the back, which is all a man like you deserves."

FOURTEEN

"If I'd have killed Wesley in cold blood like Finnegan claimed, I'd deserve to die here at your hand," Dalton said with his chin raised. "But that's not the way it happened."

Finnegan snorted his disbelief while Rocky took a step backward to stand directly behind him, his shadow showing that he'd drawn his gun.

"Dalton claimed you killed my brother, Finnegan," Rocky said. "I had intended to come to Wilmington Point to kill you, and once I've dealt with Dalton I may still do that, so explain yourself and do it well."

"I don't need to explain myself here," Finnegan said. "Talk to Sheriff Coleman. He knows the full story and he accepted that I had nothing to do with the shooting."

"Yet he didn't arrest Dalton."

"I don't know what went on between the sheriff and Dalton, but I got the impression that when Dalton offered to infiltrate Dutch Kincaid's gang, he accepted that his notoriety might give Dalton a good cover story."

Dalton shook his head, but Rocky's shadow jerked around to face him.

"Finnegan's explained himself. Now tell me the truth, Dalton."

Dalton spread his hands. "Finnegan's already done that. Talk to Sheriff Coleman and he'll confirm what happened."

"As I've told you, I've had dealings with the sheriff before and I doubt he'd go out of his way to get justice for my brother."

"He may have problems with you, but he's the kind of lawman who seeks the truth no matter who the victim is."

"Maybe he is, but right now I'm looking at you and I'm giving you one last chance to explain yourself," Rocky snarled, his harsh tone suggesting that his patience was running out.

Dalton nodded and then ran through the version of events he'd thought about providing for the last few days. As that involved laying the blame for the incident on his belief that Finnegan had drawn a gun, and right now Rocky appeared to trust Finnegan, he rejected that explanation. He couldn't think of an alternate response, but then something moved upriver and that provided him a suitable way to delay answering.

"It's a long story and you have to believe me that over the last few days I've tried a hundred times to explain it to you, but I didn't. I wish now that I had and I'll gladly talk you through the incident, but right now we don't have the time. A rider's coming downriver."

"If you don't tell me the truth, he'll see your dead body rolling into the water."

With his eyes narrowed Dalton confirmed that Vaughn was riding along the trail and he was leading a second horse with Dutch's body draped over the back. Vaughn had yet to reach the spot where they'd veered away to head up to the boulders and he was examining the ground in an intent way that suggested he was following their trail.

Dalton reckoned that following them when he knew they'd be trying to find him was just the sort of sneaky plan Vaughn would come up with, and that hunt would be coming to an end within the next few minutes.

"All right, I'll tell you what happened before Vaughn gets here," he said speaking quickly.

Rocky moved closer to the gap between the boulders and then moved back.

"You're right that it's the deputy, so be quick."

"Your brother tried to steal a wallet in the bank and then ran away. I gave chase and followed him to the side of the stable. I ordered him to stop and give himself up, but he kept going."

Dalton paused as Vaughn had drawn to a

halt, but Finnegan probably thought that he'd stopped talking before he revealed the contentious part of the story, as he grunted in anger.

"Dalton hasn't got the guts to say what happened next," he said. "He knows the moment he says it you'll shoot him."

"I agree, but I still want to hear him say the words," Rocky said.

Vaughn turned toward the boulders, although Dalton judged that as he was standing still in the shadows the deputy was unlikely to see him. Sure enough, Vaughn moved on along the lower trail, albeit more slowly than before.

"He won't," Finnegan said. "Dalton's gotten so used to lying, he doesn't know what the truth is anymore."

Finnegan's comment made Dalton snarl and with his anger growing he could no longer see the point in trying to explain the incident without mentioning Finnegan's involvement.

"Stop talking about yourself, Finnegan,"

he said. "Wesley tried to run away, but you got ahead of him and you went for your gun. Wesley panicked and reached for his own gun. I had no choice but to shoot him."

"In the back, just like you're going to die," Finnegan said.

Dalton moved back from the edge of the slope and turned to Finnegan.

"If Rocky shoots me up because I made the mistake of trying to save your life, so be it, but I sure as hell don't want to die without you telling the truth, too."

Finnegan raised his chin, wisely taking the decision not to retort leaving Rocky to raise his gun arm.

"Get back over there and turn to the water, Dalton," he said.

"Not until Finnegan admits he went for his gun and forced me to shoot your brother."

Rocky shook his head. "He doesn't have to say anything. If you'd told me this story while we were riding together, I reckon I'd have believed you, but you didn't tell me nothing other than lies until Finnegan forced you to talk."

Dalton sighed. "I know that now and I wish I had spoken up, but I didn't lie. Finnegan was responsible for what happened. If he'd stayed back or if he'd not reached for his gun, Wesley would have just run on until we managed to corner him."

"That's as maybe, but you're not denying that you're the man who shot him."

"I've shot plenty of people, and some of them to save your life, just like I did to save Finnegan, except he's too proud or too pig-headed or just too plain scared to admit that."

Rocky frowned and then lowered his gun a fraction, but the first sign that he might be prepared to seriously consider Dalton's tale made Finnegan wave an arm angrily. Then Finnegan stormed forward with a fist raised, and this time Dalton thrust up an arm to defend himself.

Finnegan still advanced on him. He slapped the arm aside and aimed a punch at him, but Dalton ducked under it and came up to deliver a sharp uppercut to Finnegan's chin that made him stumble backward for a pace. Finnegan shook off the blow and returned to deliver a flurry of punches to Dalton's chest and face that spun him around and into a boulder.

"I'm sure not scared of nothing," he said as he slapped a hand on Dalton's shoulder and dragged him away from the rock.

"Except for the truth," Dalton said. "Tell Rocky what happened. Tell him that you went for your gun and frightened his brother into going for his own gun."

"You shot him!" Finnegan roared and then slapped Dalton's face backhanded sending him stumbling on toward the gap.

Dalton stuck out a foot and stilled himself. Then he stood tall to face Rocky.

"I'm sorry for what happened to your brother, Rocky, but you must see here which one of us is telling the truth."

As Finnegan muttered an oath and advanced on Dalton, Rocky lowered his gun.

"I guess I do, but that doesn't mean I can ever trust you again," he said.

Rocky looked as if he would say more, but he'd said enough to make Finnegan's anger boil over and with a cry of defiance Finnegan charged at Dalton. With Dalton concentrating on Rocky, he was slow to defend himself and Finnegan plowed into him and knocked him backward.

Dalton tried to dig in a heel, but his foot landed on lower ground and then he was falling over backward. He just had enough time to register that Finnegan was following him over the edge of the slope before he went tumbling downward.

He tried to grab hold of something to still his fall, but the ground was too slippery, so he hunched over to protect himself and then went rolling on. The world appeared to turn over more than a dozen times before with a thud he came to a jarring halt.

The last time Dalton had seen Vaughn he'd been approaching a point below the boulders, so even if he hadn't heard them arguing, he was sure to have seen him now. Dalton shook himself, but his vision was still whirling and when he tried to sit up, his body refused to obey him and he flopped back down on his back.

He took deep breaths and tried again. This time he managed to lever himself up on to one elbow, but someone was already looming up on him in the corner of his swirling vision. He turned and found himself facing Finnegan a moment before his opponent hurled himself at him.

Finnegan caught him around the chest and knocked him on to his back. Then Finnegan launched berserk punches at him, most of which missed or caught him only glancing blows, presumably because Finnegan was struggling to orient himself as much as Dalton was.

So Dalton concentrated on prevailing while he got his strength back. Then he shoved Finnegan away and sat up quickly. The sudden motion gave him no problems and he moved to get to his feet, but he stopped when a new man loomed up closer to stand over him. Dalton raised his eyes to the man's face and then groaned.

"Deputy Vaughn," he said.

"You're lying at my feet, Dalton, which is where you belong," Vaughn said.

FIFTEEN

Dalton got up on to one knee and faced Vaughn. He still had a gun at his hip, but Vaughn had already aimed a six-shooter at his head.

"I've been waiting a long time for you to catch up with me," Dalton said. "As it looked as if you'd never find me, I thought I'd find you instead."

"Your trip down here looked like an accident to me, and you're fighting again." Vaughn smiled. "As you were losing, I reckon you and your friend should finish what you started."

Finnegan smirked and then edged his hand toward his holster, but Vaughn grunted a warning so Finnegan raised his hand. Then Vaughn gestured with his gun, and Finnegan tipped his gun out on to the ground.

Seeing no choice, Dalton followed his lead and disarmed. Then he stood up. He confirmed they had rolled to a halt close to the stretch of land where he had once tussled with Finnegan and Jebediah.

He turned back to Finnegan, but Finnegan was already making his move. Finnegan thrust his head down and stormed forward with a leading shoulder as he aimed to knock him backward and down the slope to the water in the same manner as he'd pushed him down the slope above.

This time Dalton was prepared and he leaned forward with his feet planted firmly stilling Finnegan's charge. Then he grasped Finnegan's shoulders and sought to hurl him aside. Finnegan resisted and grabbed hold of Dalton's arms so Dalton only succeeded in turning them both around.

Then they shuffled around on the spot with both men jerking themselves to either side as they sought to tip each other over. Vaughn laughed as he appraised their fight and that angered Dalton enough for him to redouble his efforts.

Finnegan resisted, although Dalton managed to bend him over at the waist, and when Dalton swung the other way, Finnegan's boots slipped on the muddy ground and he went tumbling over backward. Finnegan still had a firm grip of Dalton's arms and when he fell he dragged Dalton down with him.

Both men slapped down heavily on the ground, but Dalton landed on top of Finnegan and he pressed down. His boots and elbows skidded around as he struggled to gain traction in the mud and that gave Finnegan enough time to gather his strength.

Finnegan pressed his back firmly to the ground and then drew his legs up to plant them under Dalton's thighs. Then he kicked up. The next Dalton knew he was flying up in the air and he did a complete somersault before slamming down on his back.

He shook himself and then found that Finnegan was taking a running dive at him. Dalton rolled aside letting Finnegan splash down on his chest beside him. Then he jerked his elbow into Finnegan's kidneys making him groan before rolling over on top of him.

He sat astride Finnegan's back and he managed to pin one arm down. Finnegan still sought to raise himself with his free hand, but Dalton settled his weight on him and that stopped his opponent from moving.

When Dalton felt he was in control of the tussle, he took hold of the back of Finnegan's head and slapped it down into the mud before raising it and slapping him back down again. Then he rubbed Finnegan's face in the mud, making him splutter.

"Have you had enough?" he said, although he kept Finnegan's head buried so that he couldn't answer.

Finnegan was no longer fighting back so

he raised his head aiming to crunch it down again firmly and knock him cold, but then Vaughn hurled a coil of rope at him. The heavy object slapped him in the chest, tipping him off Finnegan and landing him on his side.

"I want to see you fight, but I sure don't want to see you win," Vaughn said as Dalton floundered.

Dalton fought his way out from under the rope and hurled it aside. Then he rose up and it was to find that Finnegan had also stood up. Finnegan was coated in mud, but clutched in his right hand was a knife.

Finnegan hadn't shown any sign of having another weapon before, but Vaughn's smirk suggested that when he'd thrown the rope at Dalton he'd thrown the knife to Finnegan. Finnegan feinted forward making Dalton step back.

Dalton noted that their fighting had moved them off the trail and they were now on the brow of the slope with Wilmington Creek thundering by below. On the other side of the trail, Vaughn had moved forward, leaving his horse and Dutch's body behind him. Finnegan turned to find out what had interested Dalton and then turned back.

"Still thinking about claiming the bounty, are you, Dalton?" he asked.

Dalton was about to ignore the taunt, but then Rocky moved on the slope behind Vaughn. When he'd last spoken with Rocky, he had appeared to be coming around to accepting Dalton's story, so he might have decided to come to his aid.

Dalton reckoned Rocky might have a chance of reaching Vaughn without being seen as the terrain provided plenty of cover. Even better, Vaughn hadn't shown that he was aware of Rocky's presence and, back at the canyon, he probably hadn't had a clear sighting of him.

In fact, when he had been in town Vaughn hadn't shown any sign that he had met Finnegan either. So he probably didn't know that he was a bank guard, and it was likely that he thought Finnegan was Dalton's partner and they were fighting over a matter connected to the bounty.

"I sure am, and so should you," Dalton said. "The moment Vaughn realizes you want the bounty as much as I do, he'll shoot you in the back."

"You're the only one here who shoots men in the back, and lawmen don't kill men like me."

"You're wrong. Vaughn's keeping his gun on both of us." Dalton lowered his voice to a whisper. "Vaughn doesn't know that Rocky is up there, so he reckons you're a bounty hunter, not a bank guard."

Dalton turned to Vaughn and then flinched with apparent shock, and that made Finnegan turn his head. That was the best distraction Dalton could have hoped to get and he charged forward.

Finnegan jerked back, his knife arm rising, but Dalton reached him before he could complete the swing and grabbed his wrist. Then he twisted the wrist and pushed the knife down bringing the two men close together.

"You lied again, Dalton," Finnegan said.

"I didn't. I thought Vaughn was going for his gun, just like I thought you were doing back in Wilmington Point."

"I was facing an armed and frightened man. What did you expect me to do?"

Dalton shook his head, accepting that for the first time Finnegan had admitted the truth that Dalton's version of events was the right one. With all the trouble that Finnegan had caused because he hadn't admitted that before, Dalton roared with anger.

Then, with his heels digging deep in the ground, he hurled Finnegan away from him. Finnegan went spinning away for two quick and uncontrolled paces. Then his feet slipped from under him.

Finnegan slapped down on his chest before he slid backward down the slope toward the water. He regarded Dalton with pleading eyes, but Dalton raised his hands. When Finnegan's slide down the slope sped up, Dalton figured that just like when he'd saved Jebediah, if he threw the rope now, he might be able to save Finnegan, but long moments passed without him acting.

Then it was too late even if he had been inclined to help him. Finnegan closed on the water's edge and with one last frantic attempt to save himself he jabbed the knife down into the dirt. The blade dug a deep furrow and it slowed him down, but he still went sliding on into the water, which instantly dragged him away from the bank.

With his arms waving frantically Finnegan drifted away until the swell on the water took him beneath the surface. After a few moments Finnegan bobbed back up, but he was lying face down in the water.

Then a strong eddy dragged him under. When several more moments had passed and Finnegan hadn't come back up again, Dalton turned away. Vaughn was facing him, his gun drawn but lowered. He had his back to the slope and Rocky was still moving behind him.

"Now there's just the two of us," Dalton

said with a confident tone. "So I guess it's time for that final showdown."

Vaughn sneered. "You don't deserve no final showdown, so I'm not giving you the satisfaction of dying here. You're coming with me."

Dalton frowned as it was now clear that Rocky wouldn't be coming to his aid as he was making his way back up the slope. Rocky was moving slowly and it took Dalton a moment to work out that he was dragging Dutch's body back to the boulders.

Clearly, while he and Finnegan had been fighting, Vaughn had kept his attention on them so Rocky had sneaked down the slope, removed Dutch's body from the horse quietly and made off with it.

Dalton smiled. "I'm going nowhere."

"From this moment on you'll do what I say, and you'll do it when I say."

Vaughn raised his gun and aimed at a spot close to Dalton's right boot. He fired, but Dalton kept his foot planted firmly on the ground.

"I sure won't," he said.

"Dance or get crippled," Vaughn said.

He fired again, and this time Dalton felt the toe end of his boot kick, but he concentrated on Rocky, who was now moving out of sight between the boulders. Rocky dragged Dutch's body beyond the edge of the slope and then stopped.

For a hopeful moment Dalton kept an eye on him, but Rocky tipped his hat and then moved back out of sight. Dalton reckoned the gesture meant that Rocky wouldn't try to help him, but he had accepted Dalton's word about his brother's death, so now he was leaving him to let justice take its course.

Dalton sighed with resignation now that he'd been abandoned, but the moment didn't last for long. With a determined gesture he moved his foot forward to the spot where the last bullet had hit the ground. He smiled and folded his arms making Vaughn scowl.

"I'm not dancing for you," Dalton said.

Vaughn muttered an oath and moved

closer, but Dalton chuckled as Rocky had now mounted up and was leading Dalton's horse with Dutch's body draped over the back. Then Rocky moved out of sight.

Dalton let his chuckling build into a laugh. Then, liking the sound, he laughed even louder.

SIXTEEN

"Quit laughing, Dalton," Vaughn said.

"I'll laugh all I want to," Dalton said, firming his jaw as he faced the deputy. "I've won."

Vaughn pointed an angry finger at Dalton. "You've got an odd way of dealing with your defeat, but as I intend to make sure you face justice, I hope that arrogance fortifies you enough to survive the long journey back to Harmony."

"You don't know the meaning of justice."

Vaughn sneered and then launched a tirade of abuse as he detailed Dalton's crime and his subsequent attempts to escape from him. Dalton didn't interrupt him, letting Vaughn enjoy gloating about his victory, as every moment that passed let Rocky get farther away.

"That smirk on your face means you don't understand what's coming to you," Vaughn said, finishing off his diatribe.

"I know what to expect so I'll enjoy my gloating."

Vaughn shook his head and beckoned for Dalton to move on toward his horse. When the deputy turned to keep his gun on him, he flinched back in surprise. Then Vaughn moved from side to side over the nearby ground, seeming to think that Dutch's body had fallen off the horse. Dalton jerked forward, hoping he might take advantage of Vaughn's confused state, but the deputy snapped back around to face him.

"What's happened to Dutch's body?" he demanded, aiming his gun at Dalton's chest.

Dalton skidded to a halt and then stood tall, but he settled his weight on his toes ready to take any chance to act that came his way.

"As I tried to tell you, I've won and you've

lost. Dutch's body has gone and you won't be claiming no bounty on it."

Vaughn winced. "There was another member of your group that I never got to see."

Dalton shook his head. "Nope. You always were a poor lawman and you got even that wrong. The man who drowned was a bank guard from Wilmington Point and my friend Rocky was hiding up there. By now Rocky should be well on his way to town with Dutch to claim the bounty."

Vaughn sneered. "He can't be much of a friend if he's left you with me."

"I accept what he's done. It's a fair result based on what I did to him."

Vaughn shrugged. Then, with a shake of the head, he appeared to accept he would struggle to catch Rocky and reclaim the body while still keeping Dalton prisoner.

"I still can't see why you're so pleased with that."

Dalton mustered a quick laugh. "Because I saw what you did at the canyon when you had to choose between checking that my body was there or claiming Dutch's body. I saw the look on your face when you found out that Rocky had gone. You wanted to claim the bounty on Dutch more than you wanted to capture me."

Vaughn nodded. "I did, but then again you always were a second-rate outlaw."

Vaughn raised his gun to sight Dalton's head and then beckoned for him to get down on his knees.

Dalton set his feet wide apart. "I accept that. I've been a bounty hunter and before that a deputy sheriff and before that a hired gun. Most importantly, before that I killed a worthless man to save others, but I've never been an outlaw."

"You can keep on claiming that right up until the moment you swing, but it's time now for you to start your new life as my prisoner, Dalton."

Vaughn edged sideways and gathered up the coil of rope he'd thrown at him earlier. Then he moved closer while again signifying that Dalton get down on his knees. Dalton turned to the slope and after a few moments Rocky came back into view downriver.

His distant form was galloping along beside Wilmington Creek. His horse and the trailing horse were throwing up a large cloud of dust and he was already over a mile away.

"Keep on going, Rocky!" Dalton yelled. "Claim that bounty on Dutch's worthless hide and enjoy every last one of those five thousand dollars!"

Rocky was too far away to have heard him and Dalton saw no sign that he would come back. Dalton didn't mind because all that mattered was that Rocky would claim the bounty and Vaughn wouldn't.

"Enjoy the moment," Vaughn said. "You won't ever again get to enjoy anything else."

Dalton shrugged and dropped to his knees. "So you've decided to take me all the way back to Harmony to receive justice, have you?"

Vaughn held out a length of rope and then

signified that Dalton should put his hands together.

"Sure, and I'll enjoy every mile of the journey knowing this rope will go around your neck when we get there."

Dalton held out his hands for Vaughn to secure him.

"Except you couldn't keep a dead body prisoner for two days." Dalton met Vaughn's eyes and rolled his shoulders. "And it sure is a long way to Harmony."

DALTON'S BLUFF

Ed Law

Dalton is facing the noose when a lucky break gives him a chance of freedom. He adopts a dead man's identity, but quickly discovers he's made a bad choice when he finds his namesake had been hired to lead a wagon train of settlers on a perilous journey to their new life.

Dalton must become the guide the settlers want him to be although he has no knowledge of the terrain or the dangers lurking ahead. And as if that wasn't bad enough, the notorious Spitzer gang is on their trail, a mysterious stranger may know his identity and one of the settlers is a killer.

With the odds so stacked against him, can Dalton pull off the greatest bluff of his life?

6th in the Dalton Series

Made in the USA
Las Vegas, NV
09 December 2021

36900209R00121